The New Impenetrable Secret *or* Polite Puzzle:
A card game from the time of Jane Austen.
Did she play it? Did it influence her work? Does it exist?

The quick, if glib answer, to the last question is, 'Well, it does now.'

The *New Impenetrable Secret* or *Polite Puzzle* was a set of ten literary text-cards, with the apparent capability of being transmitted mentally from one person to another. It consisted of 100 sentences, 'sentiments' or maxims, which were grouped in one significant way on the card-fronts, and in another on the backs.

The 'sentiments' were entirely from Samuel Richardson's novels, which Jane Austen read, admired, made fun of; but continued to allude to. Many of her turns of phrase, attitudes of mind, narrative moves – and several novel-titles – are to be found there.

The card game went through at least nine editions between 1760 and 1785. It then disappeared without trace.

This re-created version recently flummoxed a group of IT Professionals, schooled in encryption. 'Is that all?' was their response to the Explanation. Simple when you know how.

✶

In 2006 Donald Measham published *Jane Austen out of the blue* – 'a brilliant idea,' according to D M Thomas, 'brought to fruition with charm, elegance and wit.'

Here now is the promised companion to that novel. The short piece of expository fiction in the present work was once connected with the earlier one, but *Jane Austen and the Polite Puzzle* is entirely new and self-contained. It is the product of research, pondering and literary reconstruction from more than thirty years; a book which is part documentary, part well-grounded conjecture.

Donald Measham lives in Derbyshire. He was for many years managing editor of the well-regarded UK literary journal, *Staple*. After retiring from the post of Head of the School of Humanities at Derbyshire CHE (now Derby University), he returned to his own writing.

His novel *Jane Austen out of the blue* (2006) is followed by the present *Jane Austen and the Polite Puzzle* which combines fiction with documentary re-creation. In that respect, it has a similar purpose to *Lawrence and the Real England*, which Donald Measham devised for the Nottingham D H Lawrence Festival of 1985. His best-known compilation, however, remains *Fourteen*, a classic collection of writing from teenagers whom he taught, which was also translated into Italian, as *Quattordicenni* (Nuova Italia Press).

Previous published work: *Fourteen* and *English Now and Then* (both Cambridge University Press); *Leaving*, *The Personal Element* and *Larger Than Life* (Hutchinson); *Sentiment and Sentimental Psychology in Jane Austen* (offprint, R&M Studies), *Ruskin: the Last Chapter* (Sheffield Arts); *Lawrence and the Real England* and *Twenty Years of Twentieth Century Poetry*, ed. with Bob Windsor for Staple – likewise 60 monographs, collections, issues of *Staple New Writing* 1983-2000; *Jane Austen out of the blue* (Lulu).

Jane Austen
and the
Polite Puzzle

DONALD MEASHAM

www.lulu.com

ACKNOWLEDGEMENTS

I would like to thank Joan Measham for believing in this work and for her encouragement and constructive criticism. As with my previous Lulu book, I am deeply indebted to Jon Measham for his comprehensive technical support.

Over the last couple of years I have been sustained by the interest and comments of old friends and new. I would like to record my appreciation; together with a special mention of recent reactions and helpful suggestions from David Duncombe and Ulf Goebel.

Overall design control is once again by Bill Berrett. My thanks are due to him – as so often in our association – for many fine touches. The front cover is after a Rowlandson drawing made before 1820.

'The New Impenetrable Secret; or Young Lady and Gentleman's Polite Puzzle'... One deck sold for *6d*; another 'printed on superfine Cards in red and black with elegant Borders,' sold for a shilling...The bookseller, R. Withy, offered a large allowance to schools!
William M Sale Jr

By the Advice of all her Friends, she undertook what she was so well qualified for; namely, the Education of Children. But as she was moderate in her Desires, and did not seek to raise a great Fortune, she was resolved to take no more Scholars, than she could have an Eye to herself, without the Help of other Teachers...
Sarah Fielding, *The Governess* 1749, still in print 1903

'If other children are at all like what I remember to have been myself, I should think five times the amount of what I have ever yet heard named as salary on such occasions, dearly earned.'
Jane Austen, *Emma*, 1816

Contents

Introduction

Jane Austen compared herself to a miniature-painter, who worked on a 'little bit (two inches wide) of Ivory.' The *Polite Puzzle* was not dissimilar; consisting of ten 'entertaining cards' and an 'Explanation of the Secret'. Ten cards, 3¼ inches by 5¼, each with ten engraved texts on front and back. It was a mind-reading word-game, current when Jane Austen was a girl. What she may have made of it, and made out of it, is the subject of the present work.

The Contents page indicates the substance of this short book. On page 107 there is a complete set of the 'Jane Austen' cards; two of which also appear on the back cover, with the original colour-coding. Accompanying the cards is the 'Explanation of the Secret', a solution to the puzzle – which it is hoped readers will not turn to until they have tried to work it out for themselves.

In spite of the Contents page, the puzzle itself may be the best starting point for some readers. And, for those uninterested in Jane Austen, maybe the finishing point too. (The first third of 'The Puzzle in Practice' – say pages 13 to the top of 49 – provides help towards a solution, without entirely giving the game away.)

The New Impenetrable Secret or *Young Lady and Gentleman's Polite Puzzle* (its full title) seems to have been the initiative of a bookseller, R Withy, who in 1760 linked an existing word game called 'The Impenetrable Secret' with an anthology, *A Collection of Sentiments*, extracted by Samuel Richardson from his own novels. The former provided the tricky structure of the game, the latter its content.

The dates fit; so it is quite possible that Jane Austen knew well both cards and texts before her teens: memorisation is at the heart of the game. There is, however, a problem. 'The New Impenetrable Secret' lived up to its name and disappeared some time after 1785.

So the game-puzzle, described, reproduced, and played in the following pages, is a reconstruction – but one which stands upon the original foundations. Content and manner of play are true to period. I believe it provides an entertaining clarification of Jane Austen's intentions in several novels. There is a commentary[1] upon the Richardson texts used: not esoteric, requiring only a sense of the relationships in *Pride and Prejudice* and of the situation of *Persuasion*.

Beside that, it is hoped that the book will contribute to the continuing reassessment of Samuel Richardson's place in Jane Austen studies – particularly of the concise *A Collection of Sentiments*[2] which he himself extracted from the 'prolix' narrative of his novels.

Jane Austen's work is set firmly in what was for her the present time. Though she saw that some things which had changed might have been better left alone, she consistently presented the English Home Counties as more civilized than in times past and reasonably resistant to cultural fads. Since her experience of the life of other people was more limited than, say, Fanny Burney's, Austen is necessarily reliant on secondary evidence and existing documentation. Her characters read real books, quote living poets, visit actual places, write numerous convincing letters, and even become the dramatis personae of a genuine and less-than-innocent play. Some editions of *Mansfield Park* reprint the text of 'Lovers' Vows', to illustrate exactly what was going on in Sir Thomas Bertram's absence; and *Northanger Abbey* is frequently thought to require supplementary extracts from the Gothick novels which Catherine Morland devoured (as did Jane Austen, the reader) but which were lampooned by Jane Austen, the author.

It is useful to note that Austen's satire is quite often – even, usually – directed at things she herself admired and enjoyed; which does not mean that the satire is soft, rather that it is double-edged, ironic. Consider, for example, her early treatment of Richardson's *Sir Charles Grandison*. By all accounts this was her favourite book –

[1] Page 83.
[2] It contains some 6,000 classified and cross-referenced entries.

certainly, her favourite book for family reading – yet she re-wrote it in her girlhood as a squib of a theatre comedy, in which Harriet Byron, to forestall an odious suitor and a bogus marriage, throws the only prayer book onto the church's open fire during the ceremony. (It is just as curious, in our own time, that the celebrated film-makers, James Ivory and Ismail Merchant, chose to turn Jane Austen's odd little play, 'Sir Charles Grandison, or the Happy Man', into an even odder little motion picture.)

Heroines get similar bruising treatment. She poked fun at the very idea of them, listing their qualities and occupations; the regimen they had to follow, the quotations they had to learn, the lines of conversation they had to sustain. Austen was ostensibly dismissive of romantic ideas and ideals such as soul-mates (until she wrote *Persuasion*, first attachment is always first folly). Yet she, of all the classic English writers, survives as the great provider of acceptable accounts of true love: romantic love. Romantic Love, heightened rather than diminished by such observations as Elizabeth Bennet's, that she began to love Darcy a little on 'first seeing his beautiful grounds at Pemberley'. The thing is, that with so much that is rendered ridiculous, the small remainder that can survive her wit comes over as *real*. It has to be, to have passed such an acidic acid test.

Jane Austen similarly makes fun of the business of reading and itemising extracted wisdom. Mary Bennet, for example, is an owl: a dim copyist of whatever is generally accepted as constituting wit and wisdom. However, as with the business of being romantic or obsessed with Gothick, a fellow obsessive is best equipped to identify another. The consequent understanding of how a hint of a particular kind of antiquity can give the likes of Catherine Morland (*Northanger Abbey*) an agreeably disturbing frisson, is of the same order as knowing the tricks of antithesis, bathos and all that. Knowing, probably without a care for rhetoric, knowing exactly how aphoristic sentiments make their point enables Austen to take them apart, and put them together again in a manner which retains their manner but subverts their intention.

For instance, Richardson's conservative observation 'A man

may stand a chance for as good a wife among those who have fortunes, as those who have not' would have been appreciated by Jane Austen both for its unconscious comedy and for its romantic alternatives. She would have seen it in two ways: as a good rule of thumb for *Elizabeth* (who does well to marry money), but not for Darcy himself, who has no need of additional fortune: with, of course, the added complication that he's not going to be accepted on the terms he proposes.

This particular maxim may even have led to the most famous of Austen's variations on the sentimental aphorism, which comes, of course, at the very beginning of her most famous book: 'It is a truth universally acknowledged, that a single man in possession of a good fortune must be in want of a wife.'

This is a self-evidently partisan 'universal truth', which shows the female of the species, as did Shakespeare and Shaw, as agents of the Life Force – or of the selfish gene. So here is serious business, with a sanctimonious sound to it, but through the ludicrous anti-climax after the pause, and its ridiculous chief proponent (Mrs Bennet), we are warned not to take the pronouncement seriously. Not at this point: no need to, because *Pride and Prejudice* as a whole will demonstrate the security of its truth.

Small-scale structures such as this impeccable opening are not in any sense mechanical; are variations on a mechanism, rather. Austen's mastery of them goes back to her early reading, of – in particular – Richardson.

Conveniently for my purposes, and neglected by scholars, there is a curious work of 1755, called *A Collection*. In it Richardson brought together his own alphabetical indexes to his three vast novels. The resulting reference book, a kind of moral primer, had disappointing sales. By contrast (I return now to my main business) there was a highly successful by-product. I refer to the popular, but now forgotten, word-game called *The New Impenetrable Secret*, or *Polite Puzzle*. With its Richardson sentiments from *A Collection*, it went through numerous editions between 1760 and 1785.

The Puzzle in Practice

A few years before the cards were first advertised Richardson had included in his *Collection* some of the more forthright views attributed to his virtuous and upwardly-mobile servant girl, Pamela, from the novel which bears her name. For instance: 'Women in their education are generally forced to struggle for knowledge like the poor feeble infant who is pinioned, legs, arms, and head on the nurse's lap.'

Not quite so the females in the following short didactic piece of my own composition. They are, clearly, privileged. Still, their roles (which the game helps define) are constrained; particularly so in the case of the governess, who has suffered an economic and social decline (by definition: she wouldn't be a governess otherwise).

In the world of Jane Austen's novels, becoming a governess ranks high in the scale of disasters: so much so that, to the best of my recollection, it never actually happens. Charlotte Lucas's marriage to Mr Collins, for instance, ranks below even the *prospect* that elegant but needy Jane Fairfax may be obliged to leave home on such a barely-mentionable basis. The difference between the two ladies is that Miss Lucas, as Mrs Collins' wife, will have an establishment of her own (with the prospect of a male child of hers inheriting the Bennet's family home). Jane Fairfax, on the other hand (even for a salary which seems munificent to Miss Bates), would live in some other person's house as a hireling ambiguously placed between family and domestic staff.

(And Jane Fairfax might, as in Richardson's novels, have faced unwanted attentions from the head of that family. Fortunately, a convenient death enables her secretly-affianced Frank Churchill to cease his dithering. Thus, Jane Fairfax is saved at the eleventh hour.)

She would not have had to be a governess to come across *The New Impenetrable Secret*, or *Polite Puzzle*. But it would have been part of a governess's stock in trade. It was an educational tool, 'designed...to establish the Principles of Virtue and Morality in the Minds of both Sexes.' So in the following narrative I have included a governess. Contrary to Jane Austen's practice, though, I have presented her as the only personage with whom we might concern ourselves. Her charges are there to demonstrate how the puzzle is solved, how the game is played.

So, two young ladies – cousins – are with their Miss Pickering, who is six or seven years their elder. It is a wet morning in high summer and their walk is delayed.

They are playfully listing their acquaintance, and their acquaintances' acquaintance, but without much energy. The name of a personage is spoken: for example, the name acquired on marriage by Miss Elizabeth Bennet. Fiction from the period has more currency now than fact.

Says the one young lady in response to the other: 'She's a very famous lady.'

'Indeed,' says the second, 'though no longer much at court.'

'Times will change,' says the governess.

The first young lady sees that she's supposed to avoid the topic of King George's afflictions and continues: 'They say she has the ear of the queen.'

(The king is just about alive – and Jane Austen dead. So the date must be 1818 or 1819.)

The second young lady responds to the first by repeating some thing she has heard, some thing about a respectable English family being 'two necks away' from the troubles in France. She has observed that this remark has a spectacular effect when passed from lady to lady.

Only the governess understands what is being said. The reference is to a Hampshire clergyman, married to a former Miss Hancock, who became the wife and widow of a French vicomte guillotined in the Terror. The clergyman was Jane Austen's favourite brother, Henry. The governess coughs, and pulls from her sewing basket a small folder containing cards. Ten of them.

Since,' she says, 'you are in a mood for games, Miss Lucinda, why do you not entertain your visitor with these? Once very popular. A set of ten cards. I'll lay them on the table, black side up, One, Two, Three, Four, Five, Six, Seven, Eight, Nine, and TEN.' [1]

✳

---

[1] Card headings from Richardson's *Collection.* See page 80.
In the present section, = black side, ▨ = red side.

Marriage

●	*Let a man do what he will with a single woman, the world is encouragingly apt to think Marriage a sufficient amends*
●	*Exalted qualities may be sunk in a low and unequal marriage.*
●	*It is neither just nor honest to marry where there can be no love.*
●	*How unhappy must be that Marriage in which the husband can have no confidence in the love of his wife.*
●	*A prudent man will not wish to marry a woman who has not a heart to give.*
●	*Marriage is the highest state of friendship.*
●	*Marriage is a state which ought not to be entered into with indifference on either side.*
●	*In unequal Marriages, those frequently incur censure, who more happily yoked might be entitled to praise.*
●	*It is happy for giddy men, as well as for giddy women that ceremony and parade are necessary to Wedlock.*
●	*It is not a disgrace for a woman to be supposed to know something.*

Courtship

●	*The same man or woman cannot be every thing that is desirable.*
●	*Fortune is the last thing talked about by him who has none: love, love, love is all his cry.*
●	*A good estate gives a man confidence in Courtship.*
●	*A man may stand a chance for as good a wife among those who have fortunes, as among those who have none.*
●	*A worthy woman will not give hope to a man she means not to encourage.*
●	*It is not honourable for a woman to keep a man in suspense when she is not in any herself.*
●	*A single man may sometimes, in the behaviour of a daughter or sister, see that of the future wife.*
●	*A sensible man will address a woman as a woman, not as a goddess.*
●	*What additional pleasure must a woman have, who is addressed by a man of merit, and with the approbation of all her friends.*
●	*The man who is fond of his own person is not likely to be more fond of that of his wife.*

Patience, Absence, Charity

- Those who have not deserved ill-usage have reason to be easier under it.

- Solemn impressions that seem to weaken the mind may, by proper reflection, be made to strengthen it.

- Good motions wrought into habit will yield pleasure at a time when nothing else can.

- Absence from the beloved object is a cure for hasty love.

- People deeply in Love generally think too highly of the beloved object, and too lowly of themselves.

- Presence may sooner effect the cure for hasty love than absence when the object is unworthy and the female prudent.

- Charity is not extended indiscriminately.

- A generous mind, when it grants a favour, will do it grace.

- The power of doing good to worthy objects is the only enviable circumstance in the lives of people of fortune.

- Where the power of doing a beneficent action is wanting, there is nearly as much merit in the will to do so.

Generosity

●	*Judgments of person's tempers are to be made by their domestic behaviour, and by their treatment of their servants.*
●	*People in low stations have often minds not sordid.*
●	*It becomes not gentlemen to treat with insolence people who by their stations are humbled beneath their feet.*
●	*A generous spirited woman, to be happy, should take care not to marry a sordid man.*
●	*A generous mind will love the person who corrects her in love the better for the correction.*
●	*A generous person highly praised will endeavour to deserve the good opinion of the applauder, that she may not at once disgrace his judgment and her own heart.*
●	*A generous spirit cannot enjoy its happiness without communication.*
●	*The man who would be thought generous must first be just.*
●	*A generous mind will not take pleasure in vexing even those by whom it has been distressed.*
●	*A Person of a mind not ungenerous, will rather be sorry for having given a offence than displeased at being amicably told of it.*

Persuasion, Parents, First Love

●	*Persuasion strongly urged by parents is more than compulsion.*
●	*There may be cruelty in Persuasion.*
●	*Persuasion applied to a soft and gentle temper has a further cruelty to it.*
●	*Persuasion is at its most cruel when it seeks to make a worthy young creature accessory to her own unhappiness.*
●	*Parents ought to be made acquainted with any address made to their daughters before liking has taken root in Love.*
●	*First Love is generally first folly.*
●	*Wise and experienced people will not allow of that sacredness which young people are apt to imagine in a First Love.*
●	*The woman narrows her own use and consequence, who resolves, if she have not her First Love, never to marry.*
●	*Early Marriages are by no means to be encouraged.*
●	*Young people should be allowed time to look about them.*

Love

●	*Love that deserves the name obliges the Lover to seek the satisfaction of the beloved object more than his own.*
●	*Love takes deepest root in the steadiest minds.*
●	*A man or a woman may have as good a chance of happiness in marriage, with a person of fortune, as with one who has not any.*
●	*Love will acquit where Reason condemns.*
●	*A prudent person will watch over the first approaches of Love.*
●	*It is a degree of impurity in a woman to love a sensual man.*
●	*Violent Love is a fervour, like all other fervours that lasts but a little while.*
●	*True Love is fearful of offending.*
●	*Love is not naturally a doubter.*
●	*The proof of true Love is respect, not freedom.*

Learned Women

●	*Is it a necessary consequence that that knowledge which shall make a man shine, must make a woman vain?*
●	*A learned woman, with her own sex, is as an owl among the lesser birds.*
●	*Men generally are afraid of a wife who has more understanding than themselves.*
●	*Women should not be afraid either of their talents or acquirements.*
●	*Women who have talents should only take care not to give up their domestic usefulness for Learning.*
●	*Young women who are writers, should not suffer their pen to run away with their needle.*
●	*Love of reading ought not to interfere with that housewifery which is indispensable in the character of a good woman.*
●	*It is the most cruel of fates for a woman to be forced to marry a man whom she in her heart despises.*
●	*A young woman will rather choose to distinguish herself by her discretion and prudence than by her wit and poetry.*
●	*The easy productions of a fine fancy in a woman confer no denomination which is disgraceful; but very much the contrary.*

Prejudice and Pride

●	*Early-begun Antipathies are not easily eradicated.*
●	*Those we dislike can do nothing to please us.*
●	*An extraordinary Antipathy in a young Lady is generally owing to an extraordinary prepossession.*
●	*Prepossession in a Lover's favour will make a Lady impute to ill-will and prejudice all that can be said against him.*
●	*Prejudices in disfavour generally fix deeper than Prejudices in favour.*
●	*Pride, in people of birth and fortune, is not only mean, but needless.*
●	*Distinction and quality may be prided in by those to whom it is a new thing.*
●	*The contempt a proud great person brings upon himself is a counterbalance for his greatness.*
●	*There may be such an haughtiness in submission, as may entirely invalidate the submission.*
●	*A person who distinguishes not may think it is the mark of a great spirit to humour his own Pride, even at the expense of politeness.*

Sensibility, Friendship in Women, Judgment

●	*Young women ought to take their rules from plain common sense and not from poetical refinements.*
●	*Young women deeply read in romances are apt to find in their own bosoms emotions and fervours in passion.*
●	*Reading romances may leave a young woman blind to the qualities of the worthy man recommended to her.*
●	*If the second man be worthy, a woman may be happy who has not been indulged in her first fancy.*
●	*The finer sensibilities make not happy.*
●	*Friendship should never give a bias against judgment.*
●	*Two young women who are firm friends should each see something in the other to fear as well as to love.*
●	*An error against Judgment is infinitely worse than error in Judgment.*
●	*She who acts up to the best of her Judgment has the less to blame herself for, though the event should prove unfavourable.*
●	*The eye and the heart, when too closely allied, are generally at enmity with the Judgment.*

Parents and Children

- Good-nature is the characteristic of Youth.

- Some children act as if they thought their Parents had nothing to do, but to see them established in the world, and then to quit it.

- Daughters at marriageable age (whatever some of them think) have more need than ever of the care and advice of Parents.

- Modesty never forgets duty.

- The loss of a good mother is a call upon the prudence of a worthy daughter.

- Where duty to a Parent is wanting all other good qualities are to be suspected.

- Children should not be allowed to enter too early into discourse with grown people.

- It is not every woman who will shine in a state of independency.

- Children's faults are not always their own.

- Sweet to a gentle temper are the chidings of paternal love.

✳

What,' says Lucinda brusquely – Lucinda Melgrove, 'that old thing? Miss Martha will know already all there is to know about it.'

Martha– peering at the cards – does not answer.

'I'm very sure we once had a set of these,' says Lucinda – picking the cards over – 'I do think these have the same words on them.'

Martha is still not sure how to respond. Then Lucinda sees fear of having forgotten something fade from her cousin's eye, and be replaced by a glint of mild expectation. So she gathers up the cards:

'Well, if it really is a mystery to you, we'll have a session,' she continues, remembering some patter – 'Secret session. When you have been inducted into the sisterhood of the baffled, you will be amazed to find that I am able to read your mind. Prepare yourself!'

There is a long pause, unbroken by Martha, who seems impressed by her cousin's air. Lucinda, sensing that, sensing what is expected of her, suddenly seems less in charge, less grown up. Her mother is dead. She half-apologises to Martha, half-turns to the governess:

'Before we start properly,' says Lucinda, 'the game itself is clear in my memory. But these sayings on the cards, Miss Pickering – I used to know, but I've forgotten. What are they?'

'They are sentiments, Miss Lucinda,' replies the governess (who is aware that her own background is at least as good as Lucinda Melgrove's), 'though I think the term is becoming *démodé*.'

'They are from some old book, then. May I see?'

'They are from a book – or, rather, books. Old books but some would say the best books,' says the governess, recollecting the treasures of her own father's library, now dispersed.

'I have their cover here,' says Miss Pickering, handing it to Martha, 'with its rather excitable description.'

THE NEW IMPENETRABLE SECRET
OR
Young Lady and Gentleman's Polite Puzzle

An entire new Set of Entertaining Cards,
Neatly engraved on Copper-plates.

Consisting of moral and diverting Sentiments,
Extracted wholly from the much admired
Histories of Pamela, Clarissa, and Sir Charles Grandison.

The whole designed, while they amuse and entertain,
To establish the Principles of Virtue and Morality
In the Minds of both Sexes.

printed on superfine Cards in red and black with elegant borders

Published as the Act directs, 9th edition,
5 January 1771, by R. Withy.

'No,' says Martha, I've definitely not come across this before. Perhaps the Secret – whatever it is – is so old that it's taken on a sort of freshness.'

'The Secret is no more than a trick,' Lucinda replies, 'The actual writing on the cards – the sentiments – I like better than the trick. (Don't you, Miss Pickering?) They're meant to teach you rules of behaviour, but for me they always felt more like   the beginnings of ideas for stories.'

Miss Pickering knows that she should pretend to prefer that they keep to the texts as they are and the values they inculcate:

'They will do you no harm,' she declares. 'As the description of the cards tells us, they are taken from the work of the late Mr Richardson, celebrated by Dr Johnson as "father of the English novel"... Mr Richardson's writings are still my own dear mama's constant companion; and I believe he is being widely read again, thanks to *The British Novelists* series, and the industry of Mrs Barbauld.'

'I do believe,' says Lucinda, 'father has some of those big books on his shelves. Mightn't we perhaps both borrow one, and take it in turns to read to each other?'

To which the governess replies carefully: 'Your father's library is not my domain. In principle, it is not. Besides, there are works, even amongst those edited by worthy Mrs Barbauld, which your father may prefer to reserve for his own use for a while yet.'

'Such as?' says Lucinda, boldly – too boldly.

'Really, Miss Lucinda, you should not question me in that way – and certainly not (for you do so by implication) the excellent judgment of your parent.'

'I'm truly sorry, Miss Pickering, you are right, of course.'

The governess nods (pleased that her rebuke has not been challenged), and Lucinda is about to continue with the cards, when a thought occurs to her:

'I believe I have already read – with father's permission, of course – a little of the work from the *Novelists* series. Could you perhaps tell me the title of one of the books edited by the, as you say, worthy Mrs Barbauld, which you believe to be unsuitable?'

'Really, Lucinda,' says Miss Pickering, 'this is another way of questioning my judgment.'

'Pardon me, Miss Pickering, I don't believe it is. You like us to have plenty of facts. Please, simply tell me the name of the book and who wrote it, and I will ask you no more.'

'Very well,' (Miss Pickering is not sure that she is as fond of Miss Lucinda as formerly, now she is emboldened by the presence of a cousin), 'but, Miss Lucinda, let it rest after that. I had in mind *The History of Tom Jones, A Foundling* by Henry Fielding, which is not perhaps appropriate for the entertainment of young ladies – young ladies of your age. Still. Not yet. Now, if you please, to the cards. It is a game, but it has its point.'

Very well, ' says Lucinda, looking at the weather. 'I'm sorry. We'll make a proper start.' She picks up the cards from the table. 'I shall read your mind,' she says, a trifle uncertainly.

The cards feel unfamiliar in her hands, but suddenly she recalls, whole from the past: '*When any person has a mind to choose a sentence, spread the cards in your hands with the black sides uppermost. And in that manner let the person draw one.*' [1]

Martha, accepting the unspoken invitation, reaches for several.

'You must decide on one,' says Lucinda (pleased after all to be leader). Yes, look at the black side. Don't turn it over. Don't peep. The red side comes later.'

Martha reads silently. 'Some of this is quite witty,' she says.

[1] Here, and in one or two other places, Lucinda refers to the 'Explanation'.

'And some of it is not,' replies Lucinda, though actually addressing Miss Pickering.

'No,' says the governess interposing, 'not in the sense you mean – the sentiments are nicely turned. It makes them easy to remember and to find again.'

'But – *I* was going to say "but",' adds Lucinda a little pertly to Miss Pickering, and then to Martha, 'It is from some old book, while we in our present time see things differently.'

'Very true, Miss Lucinda, *but*,' the governess reminds her, ' I'm not sure we're to be accounted the better for that.'

'Oh come, Miss Pickering,' says Lucinda, 'it was the week before last, wasn't it, that I caught you – I'm sorry, but – yes – you looked as if you'd been caught; when – very well, I happened to notice that you were reading a modern French novel?'

Miss Pickering has to remind herself that, with the untimely death of her father, she has lost any claim to equality, even, with this girl.

'I was reading it, as you should be aware, solely to increase my French vocabulary.'

Lucinda exchanges a glance with Martha, who successfully represses impertinence: they concentrate on the game.

'I've read what's on the card twice,' says Martha. 'What must I do next?'

Persuasion, Parents, First Love

●	*Persuasion strongly urged by parents is more than compulsion.*
●	*There may be cruelty in Persuasion.*
●	*Persuasion applied to a soft and gentle temper has a further cruelty to it.*
●	*Persuasion is at its most cruel when it seeks to make a worthy young creature accessory to her own unhappiness.*
●	*Parents ought to be made acquainted with any address made to their daughters before liking has taken root in Love.*
●	*First Love is generally first folly.*
●	*Wise and experienced people will not allow of that sacredness which young people are apt to imagine in a First Love.*
●	*The woman narrows her own use and consequence, who resolves, if she have not her First Love, never to marry.*
●	*Early Marriages are by no means to be encouraged.*
●	*Young people should be allowed time to look about them.*

✳

'You must choose one of the sayings,' says Lucinda…

Before her cousin has finished Martha is already saying: 'I like this one. It's *Young people should be allowed time to look about them*. Though, judging from the rest of the "Persuasion" sayings it really means don't fall in love with the first person you see. But I quite like that, because they are not going to over-persuade you either.'

'Yes,' says Lucinda, 'It is a good choice. But you shouldn't have *told* me. *I* need to tell *you*! '

'You mean you knew already which I'd chosen?'

'Not quite yet,' says Lucinda,' but, no, we don't have to start afresh. You can begin with that card, if you wish – even with that sentiment, but *I* must not be told which of the texts you have chosen.'

'Oh,' says Martha, ' very well – but if I think of two sentiments and choose one, I might end up with more than one in mind and confuse myself and cheat you! Best if I choose another card.'

'Very well,' says Lucinda, taking back Martha's card which she keeps separate, while offering the other nine.

Martha takes a card and begins to scrutinise it.

'Remember,' as Martha thinks about turning the card over, 'stick to the black side. And you don't have to be able to recite your chosen words: you've merely to recognise them if you see them again.'

Courtship

●	*The same man or woman cannot be every thing that is desirable.*
●	*Fortune is the last thing talked about by him who has none: love, love, love is all his cry.*
●	*A good estate gives a man confidence in Courtship.*
●	*A man may stand a chance for as good a wife among those who have fortunes, as among those who have none.*
●	*A worthy woman will not give hope to a man she means not to encourage.*
●	*It is not honourable for a woman to keep a man in suspense when she is not in any herself.*
●	*A single man may sometimes, in the behaviour of a daughter or sister, see that of the future wife.*
●	*A sensible man will address a woman as a woman, not as a goddess.*
●	*What additional pleasure must a woman have, who is addressed by a man of merit, and with the approbation of all her friends.*
●	*The man who is fond of his own person is not likely to be more fond of that of his wife.*

✳

'You have done that for me? You have picked one of the sayings, and are going to keep it in mind?' says Lucinda, carefully.

'Yes,' says Martha, 'and I shall by no means tell you what it is.'
She conceals the card with her hand, and presses it like a little girl into her young lady's bosom.

'That's against the rules,' says Lucinda, ' you do have to give me back the card.'

Martha complies. Lucinda, after a slight glance at the card *casually, as not to be perceived*, puts the card back amongst the others.

'It's the black "Courtship" card,' says Lucinda. 'Where it goes is immaterial,' she adds to increase the mystery. 'See' – and she gives the cards a light shuffle, before handing them all to Martha.

'Now the time has come. You are to turn them over, look at the red sides and see if you can find your chosen sentiment from amongst the hundred – there are ten red sayings, sentiments, on each card.'

Martha, now that she has the red sides to address, shows curiosity about the black ones.

'Martha!' says Lucinda, 'you've seen those already, of course you have. But if you're wondering whether the backs are different, they are. Yes, the same one hundred sentiments are used but in a different order – aren't they, Miss Pickering? Your task now is to search the red sides and find your chosen black sentiment. It's there somewhere – but could be any where, on any of these red cards. Well, you'd think it could be any where. Take your time.'

'Yes, Miss Martha, please do. There's no hurry,' interposes Miss Pickering, 'Reading them through as you search is seen as an instructive part of the exercise.'

	How unhappy must be that Marriage in which the husband can have no confidence in the love of his wife.
	A man may stand a chance for as good a wife among those who have fortunes, as among those who have none.
	Absence from the beloved object is a cure for hasty love.
	A generous spirited woman, to be happy, should take care not to marry a sordid man.
	Persuasion is at its most cruel when it seeks to make a worthy young creature accessory to her own unhappiness.
	Love will acquit where Reason condemns.
	Women should not be afraid either of their talents or acquirements.
	Prepossession in a Lover's favour will make a Lady impute to ill-will and prejudice all that can be said against him.
	If the second man be worthy, a woman may be happy who has not been indulged in her first fancy.
	Modesty never forgets duty.

'You have found your chosen words on the red side?'

'Yes,' says Martha, again holding the card against her front.

'Once more,' says Lucinda, 'I must have it back: the red card. I lay it on the table before us both. Just so! Shortly – by virtue of my special powers' (she is emulating her dead mother who initiated her into the Secret) – 'I shall embark upon a process of discovery whereby I am enabled (as I promised) to read your mind... am casting my thoughts about amongst the hundred sentiments; am travelling near and far – until' (reverting to an every-day tone) 'I am able to disclose that your sentiment offers' (a touch theatrical again) 'excellent advice:

'A man may stand a chance for as good a wife among those who have fortunes, as among those who have none.'

'Yes, I chose that one,' says Martha, 'how did you do it?'

'How did I do it?' repeats Lucinda, 'that would be to divulge an ancient secret.'

Lucinda is holding a dramatic pause.

Martha repeats her question:

'No, seriously, Lucinda, how did you do it?'

Lucinda intends to hold her silence for a second longer, but it is broken by an echo of Martha's question:

'How indeed!'

The words are spoken by someone else. Miss Pickering rises and gives a little bob at the sound of the voice – a man's.

The two girls come together in surprise, to form the kind of pretty little tableau which they know will please the speaker, and in which they take pleasure. They run towards him, Lucinda's father,

Martha's uncle. He puts down a book which he is carrying, so that they can walk him, one on each arm, to the centre of the room. Releasing himself, he draws the girls together, and steps back.

'How like your mothers you both are – like the loving sisters they were. More than alike.'

'As you were repeating the discovery lines, Lucinda – I was observing you. Working your way through the sentiments of this dear old game – Well done, Miss Pickering, I thank you... And, Lucinda, how very like you seemed – so very like. So much so, that for a moment I felt I was witnessing the return of a sweet spirit.'

'I do recall mama, father. She is often in my thoughts,' Lucinda replies. 'And now going through these old cards again, I do remember quite clearly the sound of mama's voice; and do take pleasure in recalling – and, yes, emulating – the way she went about the Discovery. So there is nothing strange about the resemblance.'

'No,' says the father, Rev Thomas Melgrove, 'or, rather, yes. There is nothing strange, but much that is concordant. The resemblance goes beyond any observed recollection. As there, now – that gesture as you smooth back your hair, the inflections of the voice you use, are not common copies – are effects of the same cause, are applications of the same platonic Idea.'

He picks up his book: 'A topic that we must look to in our reading,' he concludes briskly, as a way of wiping away a tear.

He has thought of some thing, puts his book down:

'Let me look once more at these aids to reflection (for that's what they are). I don't doubt there's something apposite.'

He takes a card.

▨	*Exalted qualities may be sunk in a low and unequal marriage.*
▨	*Fortune is the last thing talked about by him who has none: love, love, love is all his cry.*
▨	*Solemn impressions that seem to weaken the mind may, by proper reflection, be made to strengthen it.*
▨	*People in low stations have often minds not sordid.*
▨	*There may be cruelty in Persuasion.*
▨	*Love takes deepest root in the steadiest minds.*
▨	*A learned woman, with her own sex, is as an owl among the lesser birds.*
▨	*Those we dislike can do nothing to please us.*
▨	*Young women deeply read in romances are apt to find in their own bosoms emotions and fervours in passion.*
▨	*Some children act as if their Parents had nothing to do, but to see them established in the world, and then to quit it.*

He reads from it with a smile.

'Young women deeply read in romances are apt to find in their own bosoms emotions and fervours in passion.'

'Uncle,' exclaims Martha, '*I* have been instructed not to disclose the chosen sentiment! And, if my eyes do not deceive me, you've drawn it from a red side.'

'Yes, because this is nearer an answer than a question. However,' says Rev Melgrove, 'sorry to have put the card before the horse – or whatever the saying is. I will leave the dénouement of your mystery to Lucinda... '

With the book – it is quite heavy – held against his chest with one hand and the conversation from the school room warming his heart, Rev Melgrove is about to return to his study with a little wave. But Lucinda is trying to make out the title of the book..

'Yes,' he says, sensing his daughter is seeking attention, but unsure of what she has in mind, 'it is time – perhaps I was implying that in mentioning the, to me, beautiful vision – time for us to begin to read Plato together…'

'*The British Novelists*, father. That looks exciting.'

'Yes, my dear, though excitement is not the only reason to spend time amongst the projected 50 volumes.'

'Are there really so many?'

'Indeed, when the project is complete. Behind it all there is another story; one of dedication.'

'Tell us, papa.'

'Yes uncle, please do.'

'Very well, there is a lady, the widow of a dissenting minister. Her name – you may have seen it, Miss Pickering, on the title-pages of various writings – is Mrs Barbauld. Her late husband was, I'm afraid, a sad case. The lady has made admirable use of the leisure afforded her by her husband's demise. She writes poetry, and earns her bread by her love of books. What do you think of that, Miss Pickering?'

'I have come across some writing of Mrs Barbauld's, sir, but I was not aware of her present circumstances.' (Miss Pickering knows more about this lady and the late husband than she reveals.) Did she not have a school?'

'She did: along with her husband. Mrs Barbauld is free of that now; has become what some people term *bas-bleu* – a blue-stocking lady – and there are those who hold that against her.'

(Miss Pickering knows all this. Though she has met Mrs Barbauld only once, she has read her work.)

'It sounds a very frightening thing to be, papa,' is Lucinda's possibly disingenuous answer.

'Ah, but she doesn't frighten me, though I have known her but a short time,' is the Rev Melgrove's slightly skittish response.

'Now here,' he continues, 'is one of the many works she has been editing... by the late Mr Fielding. Yes, I first read it as a lad and even then it wasn't new. Thirty, forty years go by so soon: do not hasten to grow up, young ladies.'

'We won't hasten any thing, papa, I'm afraid it just happens, doesn't it?' says Lucinda.

Martha, who feels referred to, blushes. Rev Melgrove does not notice. He has embarked on a list:

'His works – Mr Fielding's, that is – together with those of Mr Richardson and Mme D'Arblay (Miss Burney, that was) have been brought before a new, and grateful, public...'

He is turning the pages looking for a passage to illustrate Fielding's power to entertain and the sagacity and taste of Mrs Barbauld. He finds some thing, wonders whether to read it out, decides not to, shuts the book.

He holds the spine up to face his eyes, mouths the title, puckers his lips in almost a kiss; turns the book towards his audience of three. It has a volume number and the short form of title, *Joseph Andrews.*

'Mr Fielding, papa,' says Lucinda, 'I think I have come across the name.'

Miss Pickering, though not referred to, feels implicated. She is well read, more so than she cares to reveal: not only in Fielding, but also in Mary Wollstonecraft. She knows more than enough to address Rev Melgrove, with some firmness beneath the necessary deference, as follows:

'I think, sir, *I* may have mentioned Mr Fielding. It arose when – excuse me, sir – I was pressed   to answer Miss Lucinda. I made it clear that it was a father's and guardian's duty and privilege to determine the extent of young people's reading.'

'Oh, I don't doubt this pair of scamps have already heard whispers about *Tom Jones,* and that you, my dear Miss Pickering, will have responded very properly to whatever these slightly naughty young people said to you. But I was thinking rather of the book which I have in my hands, written by the same Mr Fielding. Open its pages, and whoever you are, you will be likely to find some character you'd very much like to meet. Or, in my case, meet again, for I have many happy recollections of dear, good Parson Adams who walked all the way to London in search of a bookseller who might publish his sermons, which he had, alas, forgotten to bring with him! Funny how books – even books of sermons, even books within books – lose their way, or get themselves written. *Joseph Andrews,* for instance, began as satire against Mr Richardson. Began by making fun of the great man.'

41

Lucinda responds rather out of turn, because of the presence of Martha:

'Papa, I should *like* that, like to read that; particularly the making fun of Mr Richardson. Those sentiments of his are so very devoted to good behaviour.'

'And so they should be,' replies her father, with a little sternness in his voice.

Lucinda dutifully lowers her eyes: 'Please excuse me, sir.'

He gives no reply, but does not intend to hold his daughter's pertness against her.

He continues as if nothing has been said, save for confirming:

'And so they should be, but you will by and by have access to some entertaining literature. Miss Pickering and I will discuss it.'

Miss Pickering acknowledges Melgrove's attention with a smile, and continuing bemusement about the degree of *rapport* he believes himself to have achieved with Mrs Barbauld.

'Thank you, father. I very much look forward to that. We both do, don't we Martha?'

Martha gives a charming little nod, as her uncle continues:

'Yes, live in hope. Always live in hope. And, if not now, *Joseph Andrews* will be yours to read quite soon. But should I, for the best of reasons, decide *not yet*, Mr Fielding had an admirable and worthy sister, who did *not* make fun of Mr Richardson. Far from it. She admired him so much, that I wonder her brother wasn't jealous!'

He looks at Miss Pickering, who dutifully acknowledges the participation he allows her in this literary chat.

'Yes,' he summarises, 'Miss Fielding has written admirably for children.'

'Children! Are we still, then, just children? Oh father…uncle!'

'No, my dears, she wrote for young ladies, too, – Mrs Barbauld likewise – so, even if it shouldn't be Mr Fielding for the present…'

('Yes,' Miss Pickering answers him inwardly, 'yes, Mrs Barbauld has also written for children, but has the reverend gentleman any idea of Mrs Barbauld's views on matrimony? This is the rigorous lady who declared "separate rights are lost in mutual love." But she, Miss Pickering, a *governess* – the very subject of Sarah Fielding's detestable book – cannot tell this man, cannot tell any of them, any of this.)

He has started looking at *Joseph Andrews* again.

'Oh papa…uncle,' they cry, but Rev Melgrove is withdrawing.

'We'll see,' he says. 'Let me alone with the book and I'll…'

With these words he is gone.

'I do hope papa offers us *Joseph Andrews*, and immediately after that, *Tom Jones* – any thing rather than Mr Fielding's disagreeable sister.'

'I'm sure she's not so very bad,' says Martha.

And it is these words that Rev Melgrove hears. He has returned to tell them that the sun is breaking through the clouds:

'Which leads me to think, Miss Pickering, that you will all be able to take your walk eventually. That should still leave time though, Lucinda, for you and Miss Pickering to induct Miss Martha into the solution of the Puzzle, shouldn't it?'

'Yes, sir,' the governess replies for both, 'though I believe Miss Lucinda capable of clearing the way to the Discovery, unprompted.' He smiles at the significance of the word 'Discovery'; or perhaps at the idea that he might be about to assist a lady in making one.

Miss Pickering also responds silently to the idea in the air. Is it possible that Melgrove could be the object rather than the subject of Discovery?   Then she wonders whether her thoughts on his behalf are entirely centred on the blue-stockinged Mrs Barbauld – perhaps someone much younger – only half as old again as Miss Lucinda – might be a preferable co-habitant of the rectory.

'To make the Discovery will be best,' Melgrove is declaring, as if he had set up some alchemical process, 'We will meet again in my study early this afternoon for a platonic dialogue followed perhaps by the mathematics.'

'Must we, father? Having begun Plato, shouldn't we stay longer in his company?

'Yes, uncle, you are teasing, aren't you?'

'Not teasing, my dears, testing.'

'Testing *us*?'

'Not directly. I'm testing Mr Richardson's insight into mathematics for young ladies.'

(They look at him.) '*Videlicet*,' he continues:

'Early-begun Antipathies are not easily eradicated.'

Prejudice and Pride

●	*Early-begun Antipathies are not easily eradicated.*
●	*Those we dislike can do nothing to please us.*
●	*An extraordinary Antipathy in a young Lady is generally owing to an extraordinary prepossession.*
●	*Prepossession in a Lover's favour will make a Lady impute to ill-will and prejudice all that can be said against him.*
●	*Prejudices in disfavour generally fix deeper than Prejudices in favour.*
●	*Pride, in people of birth and fortune, is not only mean, but needless.*
●	*Distinction and quality may be prided in by those to whom it is a new thing.*
●	*The contempt a proud great person brings upon himself is a counterbalance for his greatness.*
●	*There may be such an haughtiness in submission, as may entirely invalidate the submission.*
●	*Distinguishing not, a man thinks himself a great spirit to humour his own Pride, even at the expense of politeness.*

✳

Miss Pickering is interrupted in a reverie on the comparative convenience and inequity of having dead mothers (the lot of these girls) against the economic disaster – example, herself – of being dispossessed on account of a dead father. She turns her face with an assumed cheerfulness from Lucinda to Martha, who is saying:

'I think it would be wise to continue the work, or uncle will quiz us. Anyway, I'm quite curious and the sky hasn't cleared yet.'

'Very well,' says Lucinda, her mother about to speak through her once more. 'We have seen the game briefly in action. Let us consider' (and now it's her *father*'s turn of phrase) 'how it works as a mechanism. The game is careful to keep the black and the red cards apart from each other. Let us go against its intentions: *We* will put them together.

'What I suggest you therefore do, Martha, is take the first sentiment from this black card and *start* trying it against the red ones. See if you can find it repeated there.'

Martha reads the words aloud: '*Let a man do what he will with a single woman, the world is encouragingly apt to think Marriage a sufficient amends.* Isn't that a very cynical remark, Miss Pickering?'

Marriage

●	*Let a man do what he will with a single woman, the world is encouragingly apt to think Marriage a sufficient amends*
●	*Exalted qualities may be sunk in a low and unequal marriage.*
●	*It is neither just nor honest to marry where there can be no love.*
●	*How unhappy must be that Marriage in which the husband can have no confidence in the love of his wife.*
●	*A prudent man will not wish to marry a woman who has not a heart to give.*
●	*Marriage is the highest state of friendship.*
●	*Marriage is a state which ought not to be entered into with indifference on either side.*
●	*In unequal Marriages, those frequently incur censure, who more happily yoked might be entitled to praise.*
●	*It is happy for giddy men, as well as for giddy women that ceremony and parade are necessary to Wedlock.*
●	*It is not a disgrace for a woman to be supposed to know something.*

'You must remember,' the governess replies, 'that such opinions will not be Mr Richardson speaking in his own person. They are likely to be the words of the villainous' (but exquisitely, dangerously engaging, she actually thinks) 'Lovelace. Mr Richardson is drawing our attention here to a distortion of the meaning of matrimony.'

Martha, in emulation of her cousin's earlier challenge to the governess, would prefer to draw Miss Pickering into a discussion of the meanings of 'matrimony' and 'distortion' in the modern French novel, but Lucinda plainly wishes to proceed.

'Now, Martha,' she says (her mother, again), 'it looks to me as if you have already located Lovelace's dubious remarks on a red card.'

▦	*Let a man do what he will with a single woman, the world is encouragingly apt to think Marriage a sufficient amends.*
▦	*The same man or woman cannot be every thing that is desirable.*
▦	*Those who have not deserved ill-usage have reason to be easier under it.*
▦	*Judgments of person's tempers are to be made by their domestic behaviour, and by their treatment of their servants.*
▦	*Persuasion strongly urged by parents is more than compulsion.*
▦	*Love that deserves the name obliges the Lover to seek the satisfaction of the beloved object more than his own.*
▦	*Is it a necessary consequence that that knowledge which shall make a man shine, must make a woman vain?*
▦	*Early-begun Antipathies are not easily eradicated.*
▦	*Young women ought to take their rules from plain common sense and not from poetical refinements.*
▦	*Good-nature is the characteristic of Youth.*

'Yes,' says Martha, 'that was easy. It happened to be the top one.'

Happened?' says Lucinda, 'happened? Are you sure of that? – That it just happened? Do you notice anything about the arrangement of the sentiments? About the way the black and the red lists relate?'

'No,' says Martha, 'well, not yet. They're not in alphabetical order.'

'Agreed, they're not. But are they in any other sort of order?'

'Obviously,' says Martha, a little impatiently, ' they're in some sort of order.'

'Well, try to see what that order is. Trace the place on the red sides of all the sentiments from this same black card – the Marriage one. That may not take as long as you think. You may prove lucky depending where your eye alights.'

'I think I am lucky today. I have found another.'

'Try a further red card to see if there is a similar placement.'

Martha does so, quickly deals with another, and another.

'I think,' she says – gleefully, 'I think that every thing on this black card – yes, there's another. I think each of the ten sentiments on this black card – every one of them – is also the first line of one of the red cards.'

'So,' says Lucinda, 'if you were to pick out any one of the sentiments from this black card and tell me that you had also found it on a red side, I would have advance knowledge that it would be the top one on that red card, wouldn't I? And so I'd be able to discover it, would have found your *sentence which was privately chosen*'.

'In which case, even I could discover someone's secret if that was all there was to it,' says Martha. 'My problem is, of course, that these are only the first sentiments from the black cards. What about the other nine?'

'The answer to your question,' says Lucinda, 'is that each black card has a secret number, showing its place in the order. Our black card containing all the sentiments from the top of the red cards has the number 1. Now,' (selecting the black side of a particular card, *casually*, again, *as not to be perceived*), this is the other end of the range.

'It begins with *Good-nature is the characteristic of Youth* – as you can see: but, as you cannot see (though you soon will) the sentences on it consist entirely of BOTTOM LINES from the red cards. Yes, Martha, I do have a means of knowing that. But, no Martha, I don't mean that there are tiny numbers hidden away. Do I Miss Pickering? No, there's nothing additional to the words – only what you can see. I suppose that's what's clever about it.'

Miss Pickering nods in agreement or to indicate that she's giving the demonstration her full attention.

'Anyway,' Lucinda continues, 'you previously found out the top lines, now you must discover the bottom ones for me – by means of this card. Yes, when you find any sentiment which is the same as these black ones *on any red card*, it will always be the last one on that red card. Do you believe me? Try.'

Martha picks up the black card, headed 'Parents and Children'.

And applies herself to the set task, placing the black card side by side with a red one – any red one, she has been assured – attending to the red's last line and looking for the same words as on the black...

Parents and Children

●	*Good-nature is the characteristic of Youth.*
●	*Some children act as if they thought their Parents had nothing to do, but to see them established in the world, and then to quit it.*
●	*Daughters at marriageable age (whatever some of them think) have more need than ever of the care and advice of Parents.*
●	*Modesty never forgets duty.*
●	*The loss of a good mother is a call upon the prudence of a worthy daughter.*
●	*Where duty to a Parent is wanting all other good qualities are to be suspected.*
●	*Children should not be allowed to enter too early into discourse with grown people.*
●	*It is not every woman who will shine in a state of independency.*
●	*Children's faults are not always their own.*
●	*Sweet to a gentle temper are the chidings of paternal love.*

'Oh,' says Martha, who has started at the top, 'I do remember the words of this first black one ('Good-nature is the characteristic of Youth') – on the red card we were just looking at. I think it was – yes, indeed it *is* – the very bottom line of the red. Though it's first on the black, it proves to be (as you said it would) the last red.'

'Try another,' says Lucinda, 'look at the bottom line on another red and trace it back to this same black.'

▨	*Marriage is a state which ought not to be entered into with indifference on either side.*
▨	*A single man may sometimes, in the behaviour of a daughter or sister, see that of the future wife.*
▨	*Charity is not extended indiscriminately.*
▨	*A generous spirit cannot enjoy its happiness without communication.*
▨	*Wise and experienced people will not allow of that sacredness which young people are apt to imagine in a First Love.*
▨	*Violent Love is a fervour, like all other fervours that lasts but a little while.*
▨	*Love of reading ought not to interfere with that housewifery which is indispensable in the character of a good woman.*
▨	*Distinction and quality may be prided in by those to whom it is a new thing.*
▨	*Two young women who are firm friends should each see something in the other to fear as well as to love.*
▨	*Children should not be allowed to enter too early into discourse with grown people.*

'The last saying is a harsh one: *Children should not be allowed to enter too early into discourse with grown people.*'

'Never mind that now,' says Lucinda. 'You found it. You knew in advance. It *is* the last one on its red card– how did you know that?'

Martha hesitates a little, but is going to get it right: 'Because it came from the black card which we have just looked at.'

'Which would that be, Martha?'

'The one which begins *Good-nature is the characteristic of Youth.*'

'Correct,' says Lucinda, 'But why can we be so sure?'

'Because,' says Martha, 'because the sentiments on that black card – all ten – are also the last ones on each of the ten red cards.'

'Well done. Exactly,' says Miss Pickering.

Lucinda pays no heed to the compliment, perhaps because the second part of it is directed at Martha. She continues competently:

'You can now see that if two of the black cards determine the position of two of the ten sentiments on each of the red cards, the other eight black cards will take care of the positions of the remaining eight from the other red cards?' .

'Yes, I think I see the likelihood of that,' agrees her cousin, 'But how can you tell which is which? I might be able to distinguish the black card which has all the top ones from the black card with all the bottom ones, but I'd never manage that sort of thing for the other eight: there would be far too much to remember. There must be some secret mark or code.'

Yes, but as I said before, it's just what you see in front of you; not a foreign body, not some old hieroglyph. Every black card has a *Catch Letter*, which is always in a special place – in one of the words in the first sentiment. Pick the right letter out of each card, put the ten of them together and they will make an acrostic. An acrostic, Martha, as I'm sure you know –'

'Only too well. Acrostics are stuck in my head, pricked in my finger. I was once obliged to work some acrostic poetry into a sampler.'

'I had to do it too,' says Lucinda. 'I expect it was the same poem…'

They start to recite in unison a poem by Sir John Davies, whose sixteen line-initials turn into a vertical tribute to ELISABETHA REGINA – decide it is too long, and in any case begin to giggle.

(Miss Pickering congratulates them both. She has quite enjoyed the last part of the dialogue between the two young ladies and considers they have done well. During the poem, though, she had drifted into a consideration of the degree of disparity of age between herself and Rev Melgrove. If he is, as he just might be, considering re-marriage, she is quite sure – and is correct in that view – that he would find herself, a member of his own household, a more feasible match, a more congenial bride, than a learned lady who has moved beyond all that sort of thing; who is hostile to domesticity, and has put on record her opposition to the very notion of formal ties between men and women.)

✳

As the governess muses, Martha is arranging the cards on the table: reading up and down, trying to cipher and decipher.

'No,' says Lucinda, watching her, 'we'll get nowhere like that. The acrostic in the Secret is not like old ELISABETHA's. This one's not based on the first word of each line. So…'

'…Then,' says Martha, supplying a conclusion, 'It's not the usual sort of acrostic, I think. Isn't there another term, Miss Pickering?'

(Miss Pickering has proved adept at her work because she has a quick awareness of her own name even when her thoughts are far away, and an ability to react to it with some accuracy.)

'What about "telestich"?' the governess replies – 'from the ancient Greek *telos*, "end"; together with *stikhos*, "line of verse".'

'Yes, thank you Miss Pickering, that's what I remember being told,' says Martha, for this was the sort of thing which governesses knew and young ladies learnt in 1818 or1819. 'The *last* letter of each sentiment, then, Lucinda? Is that how it works here?'

'Not quite,' says Lucinda, 'but close. We must hurry now. I do think (as father prophesied) the sun is beginning to break through – So let me be helpful… Suppose I list the **black cards** in order like a class in a big school, from top to bottom, according to their capacity – and then you try to *discover* how I am enabled do that,' she concludes, with emphasis on what has been a recurrent hint.

'So these are the **black** cards in their secret order. If only you could look back – look back in time, I mean – I believe it is the one in which Miss Pickering originally laid them out on the table.[1] We need just their first sentiment, so I've covered the rest. See how they begin:

'1st   *Let a man do what he will with a single woman, the world is encouragingly apt to think Marriage a sufficient amends.*

2nd   *The same man or woman cannot be every thing that is desirable.*

3rd   *Those who have not deserved ill-usage have reason to be easier under it.*

4th   *Judgments of person's tempers are to be made by their domestic behaviour, and by their treatment of their servants.*

5th   *Persuasion strongly urged by parents is more than compulsion.*

6th   *Love that deserves the name obliges the Lover to seek the satisfaction of the beloved object more than his own.*

7th   *Is it a necessary consequence that that knowledge which shall make a man shine, must make a woman vain?*

8th   *Early-begun Antipathies are not easily eradicated.*

9th   *Young Women ought to take their rules from plain common sense and not from poetical refinements.*

10th   *Good-nature is the characteristic of Youth.*'

[1] See page 16.

Martha looks the lines over:

'You are talking of an acrostic, Lucinda. But not one using first letters of lines of poetry. I shall try my idea,' she says, 'telestich. So I am taking the *last* letter of each of the first sentiments. Yes – the last letters do work: the first four of them spell out SETS –!'

'Yes, they do *seem* to be working. But after your SETS, it's nonsense,' adds Lucinda, ' Look at the next two sentiments, which produce NN! – Double N at what should be the beginning of a word? So, no, I'm afraid nothing of quite of that kind is intended. You are very, very, very close to the secret, though. Only four or five or six letters away. You've gone a little too far.'

'Very well, Lucinda, these last letters have let me down. Instead, I'll try the *initial* of the last word, as you hint!   So.'

And Martha starts to work down the list:

'<u>A</u> looks promising; <u>AD</u> is possible; but <u>ADI</u> seems unlikely...' Martha pauses, doubtful now.

'Don't be discouraged,' Lucinda urges.

'<u>ADIS</u> what kind of word is this?'

Lucinda does not answer, so Martha continues:

<u>ADISC</u> – I think I begin to see – <u>ADISCOV</u> – I do see: <u>A DISCOVER</u>– <u>A DISCOVERY</u>!'

'Hurrah,' cries Lucinda. Those ten letters are the *Catch Letters* of the <u>First</u>, <u>Second</u>, <u>Third</u>, <u>Fourth</u>, <u>Fifth</u>, <u>Sixth</u>, <u>Seventh</u>, <u>Eighth</u>, <u>Ninth</u>, <u>Tenth</u> black cards!'

'Yes, I do believe I have it: They are also examples of First, Second, Third, Fourth, Fifth, Sixth, Seventh, Eighth, Ninth, Tenth Sentiments <u>from the red cards</u>!'

'Very good,' says Lucinda, 'For completeness, I'll just write the position of each line on the left and set some capital letters to the right, so you can see them clearly…Wait a minute, we've just time, I'll take a fresh piece of paper…'

✳

Lucinda is still writing the list, taking pleasure in the clarity of her hand, which she knows Miss Pickering will inspect with approval:

'Top   *Let a man do what he will with a single woman, the world is encouragingly apt to think Marriage a sufficient **A**mends.*

2nd   *The same man or woman cannot be every thing that is **D**esirable.*

3rd   *Those who have not deserved ill-usage have reason to be easier under **I**t.*

4th   *Judgments of person's tempers are to be made by their domestic behaviour, and by their treatment of their **S**ervants.*

5th   *Persuasion strongly urged by parents is more than **C**ompulsion.*

6th   *Love that deserves the name obliges the Lover to seek the satisfaction of the beloved object more than his **O**wn.*

7th   *Is it a necessary consequence that that knowledge which shall make a man shine, must make a woman **V**ain?*

8th   *Early-begun Antipathies are not easily **E**radicated.*

9th   *Young Women ought to take their rules from plain common sense and not from poetical **R**efinements.*

Bottom *Good-nature is the characteristic of **Y**outh.*

'There it is entirely,' says Lucinda (still rather pleased with herself, rather too pleased, thinks Miss Pickering): 'A DISCOVERY. Yes, it's a sort of acrostic… Any sentiment chosen from the black <u>A</u> card will be found in first place on one of the red cards; while any sentiment chosen from the black $\underline{D}$ card will come second; $\underline{I}$ third; S fourth; and so on to $\underline{Y}$ at the bottom.

'Now, supposing the sentiment you have chosen is from the black C card' (pointing to her list) ' – whose first sentiment ends in **'C**ompulsion**'**. C is the *fifth letter* of the acrostic, indicating that each of the ten sentiments on this black card will also be the *fifth item on one of the ten red cards.* You hand a red card to me as the operator, saying your chosen sentiment is somewhere on it. As I will have already surreptitiously observed the Catch Letter **C** on the black card where you first found your secret sentiment, I shall simply count down to the fifth sentiment on the red, and read out that which was once *your* secret, but now is *my* Discovery.'

▨	*It is not a disgrace for a woman to be supposed to know something.*
▨	*The man who is fond of his own person is not likely to be more fond of that of his wife.*
▨	*Where the power of doing a beneficent action is wanting, there is nearly as much merit in the will to do so.*
▨	*A Person of a mind not ungenerous, will rather be sorry for having given a offence than displeased at being amicably told of it.*
▨	*Young people should be allowed time to look about them.*
▨	*The proof of true Love is respect, not freedom.*
▨	*The easy productions of a fine fancy in a woman confer no denomination which is disgraceful; but very much the contrary.*
▨	*A person who distinguishes not may think it is the mark of a great spirit to humour his own Pride, even at the expense of politeness.*
▨	*The eye and the heart, when too closely allied, are generally at enmity with the Judgment.*
▨	*Sweet to a gentle temper are the chidings of paternal love.*

We have it again: *Young people should be allowed time to look about them*!
'A, D, I, S, C, O, V, E, R, Y... An old thing lost and found again:
A SECRET discovered...'

Not yet Miss Pickering's. She is crossing the paddock with her
charges. She may prove an efficient step-mother and loyal wife,
after Melgrove has been rejected, wittily, by his learned lady. The
cards are left on the table; their possibilities in the air.

▨	*Let a man do what he will with a single woman, the world is encouragingly apt to think Marriage a sufficient amends.*
▨	*The same man or woman cannot be every thing that is desirable.*
▨	*Those who have not deserved ill-usage have reason to be easier under it.*
▨	*Judgments of person's tempers are to be made by their domestic behaviour, and by their treatment of their servants.*
▨	*Persuasion strongly urged by parents is more than compulsion.*
▨	*Love that deserves the name obliges the Lover to seek the satisfaction of the beloved object more than his own.*
▨	*Is it a necessary consequence that that knowledge which shall make a man shine, must make a woman vain?*
▨	*Early-begun Antipathies are not easily eradicated.*
▨	*Young women ought to take their rules from plain common sense and not from poetical refinements.*
▨	*Good-nature is the characteristic of Youth.*

▓	*Exalted qualities may be sunk in a low and unequal marriage.*
▓	*Fortune is the last thing talked about by him who has none: love, love, love is all his cry.*
▓	*Solemn impressions that seem to weaken the mind may, by proper reflection, be made to strengthen it.*
▓	*People in low stations have often minds not sordid.*
▓	*There may be cruelty in Persuasion.*
▓	*Love takes deepest root in the steadiest minds.*
▓	*A learned woman, with her own sex, is as an owl among the lesser birds.*
▓	*Those we dislike can do nothing to please us.*
▓	*Young women deeply read in romances are apt to find in their own bosoms emotions and fervours in passion.*
▓	*Some children act as if they thought their Parents had nothing to do, but to see them established in the world, and then to quit it.*

	It is neither just nor honest to marry where there can be no love.
	A good estate gives a man confidence in Courtship.
	Good motions wrought into habit will yield pleasure at a time when nothing else can.
	It becomes not gentlemen to treat with insolence people who by their stations are humbled beneath their feet.
	Persuasion applied to a soft and gentle temper has a further cruelty to it.
	A man or a woman may have as good a chance of happiness in marriage, with a person of fortune, as with one who has not any.
	Men generally are afraid of a wife who has more understanding than themselves.
	An extraordinary Antipathy in a young Lady is generally owing to an extraordinary prepossession.
	Reading romances may leave a young woman blind to the qualities of the worthy man recommended to her.
	Daughters at marriageable age (whatever some of them think) have more need than ever of the care and advice of Parents.

▨	*How unhappy must be that Marriage in which the husband can have no confidence in the love of his wife.*
▨	*A man may stand a chance for as good a wife among those who have fortunes, as among those who have none.*
▨	*Absence from the beloved object is a cure for hasty love.*
▨	*A generous spirited woman, to be happy, should take care not to marry a sordid man.*
▨	*Persuasion is at its most cruel when it seeks to make a worthy young creature accessory to her own unhappiness.*
▨	*Love will acquit where Reason condemns.*
▨	*Women should not be afraid either of their talents or acquirements.*
▨	*Prepossession in a Lover's favour will make a Lady impute to ill-will and prejudice all that can be said against him.*
▨	*If the second man be worthy, a woman may be happy who has not been indulged in her first fancy.*
▨	*Modesty never forgets duty.*

▓	*A prudent man will not wish to marry a woman who has not a heart to give.*
▓	*A worthy woman will not give hope to a man she means not to encourage.*
▓	*People deeply in Love generally think too highly of the beloved object, and too lowly of themselves.*
▓	*A generous mind will love the person who corrects her in love the better for the correction.*
▓	*Parents ought to be made acquainted with any address made to their daughters before liking has taken root in Love.*
▓	*A prudent person will watch over the first approaches of Love.*
▓	*Women who have talents should only take care not to give up their domestic usefulness for Learning.*
▓	*Prejudices in disfavour generally fix deeper than Prejudices in favour.*
▓	*The finer sensibilities make not happy.*
▓	*The loss of a good mother is a call upon the prudence of a worthy daughter.*

▦	*Marriage is the highest state of friendship.*
▦	*It is not honourable for a woman to keep a man in suspense when she is not in any herself.*
▦	*Presence may sooner effect the cure for hasty love than absence when the object is unworthy and the female prudent.*
▦	*A generous person highly praised will endeavour to deserve the good opinion of the applauder, that she may not at once disgrace his judgment and her own heart.*
▦	*First Love is generally first folly.*
▦	*It is a degree of impurity in a woman to love a sensual man.*
▦	*Young women who are writers, should not suffer their pen to run away with their needle.*
▦	*Pride, in people of birth and fortune, is not only mean, but needless.*
▦	*Friendship should never give a bias against judgment.*
▦	*Where duty to a Parent is wanting all other good qualities are to be suspected.*

▓	*Marriage is a state which ought not to be entered into with indifference on either side.*
▓	*A single man may sometimes, in the behaviour of a daughter or sister, see that of the future wife.*
▓	*Charity is not extended indiscriminately.*
▓	*A generous spirit cannot enjoy its happiness without communication.*
▓	*Wise and experienced people will not allow of that sacredness which young people are apt to imagine in a First Love.*
▓	*Violent Love is a fervour, like all other fervours that lasts but a little while.*
▓	*Love of reading ought not to interfere with that housewifery which is indispensable in the character of a good woman.*
▓	*Distinction and quality may be prided in by those to whom it is a new thing.*
▓	*Two young women who are firm friends should each see something in the other to fear as well as to love.*
▓	*Children should not be allowed to enter too early into discourse with grown people.*

▨	*In unequal Marriages, those frequently incur censure, who more happily yoked might be entitled to praise.*
▨	*A sensible man will address a woman as a woman, not as a goddess.*
▨	*A generous mind, when it grants a favour, will do it grace.*
▨	*The man who would be thought generous must first be just.*
▨	*The woman narrows her own use and consequence, who resolves, if she have not her First Love, never to marry.*
▨	*True Love is fearful of offending.*
▨	*It is the most cruel of fates for a woman to be forced to marry a man whom she in her heart despises.*
▨	*The contempt a proud great person brings upon himself is a counterbalance for his greatness.*
▨	*An error against Judgment is infinitely worse than error in Judgment.*
▨	*It is not every woman who will shine in a state of independency.*

	It is happy for giddy men, as well as for giddy women that ceremony and parade are necessary to Wedlock.
	What additional pleasure must a woman have, who is addressed by a man of merit, and with the approbation of all her friends.
	The power of doing good to worthy objects is the only enviable circumstance in the lives of people of fortune.
	A generous mind will not take pleasure in vexing even those by whom it has been distressed.
	Early Marriages are by no means to be encouraged.
	Love is not naturally a doubter.
	A young woman will rather choose to distinguish herself by her discretion and prudence than by her wit and poetry.
	There may be such an haughtiness in submission, as may entirely invalidate the submission.
	She who acts up to the best of her Judgment has the less to blame herself for, though the event should prove unfavourable.
	Children's faults are not always their own.

Walpole's Secret,
Richardson's Sentiments

Walpole's Prototype Game:

The Vices of Age are as bad or worse than Those of Youth.

Love is a credulous Thing.

Good nature is a Great misfortune when it is not manag'd with Prudence.

A Pause, an unkind Tone, Word, Look or Action, destroys the Grace of a Courtesie.

Where's Difference between yEnemy who does you no harm & tFriend who does no good?

Women are the first who discover their own Charms and fall in Love with them.

The subtlest Fetch & Dissimulation is to pretend being Caught.

A Fool knows better what is done at his Neighbour's House than at his own.

An unchaste Woman is only a Sinner, but an impudent one is a Monster.

There is less Merit in saying many Witty things, than in never saying a Foolish one.

Text of 'Y' card from *The Impenetrable Secret* (1758?)

Walpole's Secret, Richardson's Sentiments

Such games as these, games with 'sentiments', are still alive (though hardly kicking) in the mottoes and riddles of British crackers[1] and American fortune cookies. Even now they may serve as talking points and to set up little social interchanges, though the spirit of, say, eighteenth-century 'sentimental toasting' has long gone. Which is perhaps as well, for that ritual, supposedly with an element of moral uplift, had become an excuse for teasing and humiliation – particularly of young ladies, as Fanny Burney recalled:

> After supper Dr Wall gave about Sentimental toasts. We were all mighty stupid at them, and he was obliged to help every body. When my turn came I told him, that not being able to think of a *sentiment* I would give him a *good wish*, and then I drank a Fair Day to the Review To-morrow. Dr Wall pretended to misunderstand me...

And Lucy Aikin[2], born in 1781, and so six years younger than Jane Austen, described

> ...the sufferings of young ladies who were called upon by custom to drink the good health of each one at the dinner-table in *beer*... It was even worse when we came to the wine *after* dinner or supper. It was *then* not sufficient to drink healths. A young lady would often be obliged, in spite of blushes and entreaties, to give us a toast, either the name of a single gentleman, or a *sentiment*: perhaps such a flat affair as this, 'May the single be married, and the married happy.'

---

[1] Decorated tubes of coloured paper, pulled apart at Christmas time.
[2] Poet, niece of Mrs Barbauld (née Aikin).

71

That was the platitudinous, joshing era of Jane Austen's childhood. By her teens she was laying heavy hands on sentimental attitudinising: 'I entered & while the rest of the party were devouring Green tea & buttered toast, we feasted ourselves in a more refined & Sentimental Manner by a confidential Conversation. I informed them of every thing which had befallen me during the course of my Life, and at my request they related to me every incident of theirs.' This is from 'Love and Friendship', a very funny, knockabout piece, dating from around 1790.

Twenty years before Jane Austen was born, Samuel Richardson, printer and novelist, had laboriously extracted what he called 'the pith and marrow' of his novels – the memorable maxims, the guides to living, the warnings to loose-livers – and re-published them as a pocket guide to human behaviour and morality. This was the 1755 anthology *A Collection*, mentioned in the Introduction: the fuller form of its title being,

A Collection of the Moral and Instructive Sentiments, Maxims, Cautions and Reflexions Contained in the Histories of Pamela, Clarissa, and Sir Charles Grandison...

Two years after this Richardson publication, the cognoscente and Gothick innovator Horace Walpole set up a printing press at his castellated country house, Strawberry Hill. There he printed a number of short pieces in 1758, probably including the 'Explanation of the Secret' (in Walpole's type-face), which accompanied his engraved 'Impenetrable Secret' cards. Kept as a novelty in a glass case at Strawberry Hill, they were sold off in 1842; and eventually passed to the British Museum Library, now the British Library. There is no clear evidence that the cards were offered for sale nor, even, that there was ever more than this one set in Walpole's life-time.

My 1758 date for the printing is a conjectural one. But, then, so is the '1780[?]', which was recorded in pencil on an early British Museum catalogue card. That later date cannot be correct for two good reasons. (1) If Walpole is the inventor of 'The Impenetrable Secret' (and there is another museum note to that effect), it must have appeared before 1760, when the Richardson-derived 'New Impenetrable Secret, or Young Lady's and Gentleman's Polite Puzzle' was first advertised in *The London Chronicle* by R Withy; (2) Common sense indicates that the 1760 '*New* Impenetrable' set of cards would not have appeared before a title which is simply 'Impenetrable'. Modernist prequels and sequels can prove devious, but, even now, *Blockbuster I* generally appears before *Blockbuster II*.[1]

The ten cards of the original game have been kept in a small wooden box bound after the manner of a book, the inside of which bears Walpole's bookplate. The cards measure 3¼ inches by 5¼ inches. The sayings are engraved on both sides of the cards copperplate-style – one side, black, the other red: the work probably of Walpole's Swiss factotum, Mütz.[2]

    Apart from the cards, the box contains two items: a past librarian's note ('Strawberry Hill/A game invented by Horace/Walpole and printed by him at /Strawberry Hill. /Has his book plate'); and a printed sheet, twice the size of the cards, headed 'Explanation of the Secret'.

A couple of years after the production of Walpole's game (on my dating), *The New Impenetrable Secret...*or *Polite Puzzle* was launched by Withy. It went through nine editions or more. 'Extracted wholly' from Richardson – using the sentiments conveniently available from the 1755 *Collection* – it was advertised and re-advertised for 25 years (1760-1785).

    This source-book, Richardson's *Collection*, was not re-printed. But in a sense it did not need to be, because in a somewhat more condensed form it continued to exist as Appendices to the

[1] William R Sale Jr, bibliographer of Richardson, is quite clear that it was the *Collection* sentiments which were used for the puzzle, 'printed on cards, in a deck called "The New Impenetrable Secret..."'

[2] '– a painter in the house, who is an engraver too, a mechanic and everything,' (Walpole, letter 1758).

three source-novels, under the heading 'An Index, Historical and Characteristical.' Thus, in all editions of *Sir Charles Grandison* available to Jane Austen, she would have had the main headings of every section and all the references to follow up.

Also, a hundred of the sentiments from Richardson's novels continued to be read and memorised on the 'entertaining cards' of *The New Impenetrable Secret.* They remained available and were reissued from time to time until Jane Austen was ten; and sets may have continued in use until well after that.

The first edition of the cards by the bookseller R Withy was advertised in *The London Chronicle* (22nd-24th April 1760), closely followed by another on 2nd May, by the same bookseller — a second edition already? If so, it may have been occasioned by disaster rather than rapidity of sales. In this *Daily Advertiser* notice, the attribution is: 'Printed for R. Withy, book and print-seller, (burnt out from Cornhill) at the Dunciad, the corner of Rood-Lane in Fenchurch Street.'

Richardson, as already noted, had himself taken on the task of extracting and classifying the sentiments for his *Collection* ('which I once thought I could also have left to another hand'). It is quite possible that he also selected the sentiments for the card game personally. Mrs Barbauld in amending her preface to the 'British Novelists' edition of *Clarissa*, speaks of his 'assisting in a few works for book-sellers' in his later years: a passage which, maybe significantly, replaces one in which she had previously discussed *A Collection.* There is, too, in all the advertisements for the cards, a Richardsonian emphasis on establishing 'the Principles of Virtue and Morality in the Minds of both Sexes', which suggests either Richardson's hand in the enterprise or a placatory attitude towards him on the part of booksellers.

Another edition followed in December 1767, for George Pearch; also one for S Steare; and a 9th Withy edition in 1771. The popularity of this *New* educational game far exceeded that of its twin sources, Richardson's *Collection* and Walpole's prototype game, *The Impenetrable Secret.*

There may have been other subsequent British editions of the *New Impenetrable Secret...Polite Puzzle*. It was advertised again (using a slightly garbled version of the previous patter[1]) in Philadelphia on December 17, 1785. Then it disappeared; as ephemera, by definition, will.

How it was played, even, was forgotten. For instance, Mr Patrick Murray, founder of the Museum of Childhood in Edinburgh, suggested to me that it might be an example of 'Quartettes', 'a simple matching game'. Meanwhile in the British Museum the Walpole game with its related title and description of play, had rested for more than a century, apparently undisturbed, save for the making of a whimsical American facsimile in 1938.[2]

But even after the case is made for the connection between the Walpole and Richardson games[3] questions remain.

Chief among these are: (1) Can we be sure that the Richardson and the Walpole versions of *The Secret* were played according to the *same rules*? (2) Are we equally sure that their *content* was quite different?

The answer to the first question is a pragmatic 'yes', based on descriptions of the two games and a shortage of alternative viable word-mechanisms. The topic will be returned to at the end of this section.

A positive answer to the second question is more straightforward:
(a) Press notices plainly and consistently state that the sentiments used in 'The New Impenetrable Secret' are taken *wholly* from Richardson's novels.
(b) None of the 100 sentiments on Walpole's cards is attributable to Richardson.
(c) It is hardly likely that they would be, since Walpole looked down on Richardson, 'who wrote those deplorably tedious lamentations,

[1] Page 27 refers.
[2] 200 copies were printed, one of which recently appeared for sale on the Internet.
[3] D C Measham, 'Richardson and Jane Austen: A comparative Study', M Phil Thesis, Nottingham 1971.

75

"Clarissa" and "Sir Charles Grandison", which are pictures of high life as conceived by a bookseller..."[1] Unless he had wished to belittle Richardson by using his work in a game...

In the sample card examined below, those sources which can be traced are from writers other than Richardson. Attributions are regarded as probable where not queried.

(1) *The Vices of Age are as bad or worse than those of Youth.*
Ovid.
(2) *Love is a credulous Thing.*
Cicero.
(3) *Good-nature is a Great misfortune when it is not managed with Prudence.*
Machiavelli?
(4) *A Pause, an unkind Tone, Word, Look or Action, Destroys the Grace of a Courtesie.*
Orlando Furioso ?
(5) *Where's Difference between the Enemy who does you no harm, and the Friend who does you no good?*
Traditional?
(6) *Women are the first who discover their own charms and fall in love with them.*
Possibly Walpole himself – close to phrases from *The Castle of Otranto*, which these sentiments probably pre-date.
(7) *The subtlest Fetch and Dissimulation is to pretend being Caught.*
Variation on Francis Bacon?
(8) *A fool knows better what is done at his Neighbour's House than at his own.*
Spanish proverb.
(9) *An unchaste woman is only a sinner, but an impudent one is a monster.*
Sentimental toast.
(10) *There is less Merit in saying many Witty things, than in never saying a Foolish one.*
Answer to Rochester's 'epitaph' for Charles II?

[1] Walpole, letter of 1764; similar remarks in 1753.

The text of this sample black card is not merely unattributable to Richardson, it does not resemble his manner or his books – though he might have seen the point of the fourth and last sentiments.

Their cosmopolitan outlook, for instance, is not his. Nor the misogynist strain in number nine; or, for example, the crudeness of 'Women's Tempers like Faces, appear generally best at a distance', a contingent sentence on a red card.

✳

Back now to the mechanics of the two 'Impenetrable' games: to begin with the obvious, not only Walpole's game, but his 'Explanation of the Secret' is extant. It has been used to devise the re-constructed 'New Impenetrable Secret'.

Given the similarity of the two titles, the emphasis in the advertisements for the 'New' cards on their being printed in red and black, and the aphoristic nature of the texts, it would have been over-sceptical to assume that the two games would have worked quite differently. However, within acceptance of an overall similar intention, I have tried other ideas for the specifics. For instance, I wondered whether the sub-title of the game, POLITE PUZZLE, might have been used as a basis for the catch-letters, or whether the game was more elaborate than its predecessor; with perhaps triple acrostics: PAMELA, CLARISSA, and GRANDISON, maybe.

But (even ignoring the fact that having to locate as a new player, a memorised sentiment from a hundred in red print distributed over ten cards probably nears the limit of one's patience) neither of these suggestions will *work*. The acrostic A DISCOVERY, of course, has no recurring letter: both POLITE PUZZLE and the titles of Richardson's novels involve repetition of 'catch'-initials; which makes it impossible for them to determine the sequence. I therefore stand by the reconstruction I have made (as used in 'The Puzzle in Practice', above) in which ten key Richardson sentiments conceal and spell out A DISCOVERY, as they did in Walpole's original.

✳

The Austen Connection

A
COLLECTION

Of the Moral and Instructive

SENTIMENTS, MAXIMS, CAUTIONS,
and REFLEXIONS,

Contained in the

Histories of PAMELA, CLARISSA, and Sir CHARLES GRANDISON.

Digested under Proper HEADS,

With Reference to the Volume, and Page, both in
Octavo and Twelves, in the respective Histories.

L O N D O N :
Printed for S. Richardson;
And Sold by C. Hitch and L. HAWES, in *Pater-noster Row;*

M.DCC.LV.

1755 Title-page (lower half abridged)

A Collection, 'the pith and marrow' of all Richardson's works: from which the sentiments for *The Impenetrable Secret* or *Polite Puzzle* were 'wholly extracted'...

Now you have penetrated the Secret of the Puzzle – you will have an idea of the way in which the cards need to be scrutinised by the guest-players and managed by the host-operator. A quick-witted operator will be able to make a mental note of the secret 'Catch Letters' and 'read' several minds simultaneously.

You will also be in a position to consider how the cards could have been used with children in a school room. They certainly test the ability to read, remember and identify: even when the Secret is known, a good deal of sustained attention is required on the part of the 'host'. The mystery, one guesses, could be protracted by an adult operator without revealing how the Secret was to be discovered. It could be a daily marvel.

Jane Austen knew Richardson's novels well from an early age. To have a hundred small extracts from the voluminous works pass beneath her skimming eyes on the black fronts and red backs would have been an odd, but significant, experience – if it happened. One searches for an analogy from our own time.

I am old enough to have been brought up on a regimen of formal English, and remember exercises in which scraps of literature mixed with banalities were listed in text books for Subject-Predicate analysis. Among them, I recall from the age of eleven, the sentence: 'The evil that men do lives after them' which was to be set out in two columns as S and P. An inept way of approaching sentence structure, but important for me at that moment: in that somehow I recognized with excitement, without having read or seen the play, that the words were from *Julius Caesar*.

So, again, who knows what ideas might have started up in the head of a young Jane Austen, someone far more precocious and receptive? One guesses that, for example, ideas for titles might have stuck in her mind from scrambled word-play. Or, she could have recognised great chapters of Richardson in their entirety on the basis of extracted half-sentences, or whimsically juxtaposed and interjected scenes and out-of-context phrases.

Sentiments, &c. *extracted from* The *History of* CLARISSA.

Prejudice. Prepoffeffion. Antipathy.

E ARLY—BEGUN Antipathies are not eafily eradicated, i. 19. [20].

Thofe we diflike can do nothing to pleafe us, i. 89. ii. 114. [i. 92. ii. 202].

An extraordinary Antipathy in a young Lady to a particular perfon, is generally owing to an extraordinary prepoffeffion in favour of another, i. 108. [112].

An eye favourable to a Lover, will not fee his faults thro' a magnifying glafs, ii. 50. [142]

Prepoffeffion in a Lover's favour will make a Lady impute to ill-will and prejudice all that can be faid againft him, *ibid*.

Old prejudices [*tho' once feemingly removed*] eafily recur, ii. 314. [iii. 52].

To thofe we love not, *fays Lovelace, fpeaking of Mr. Hickman*, we can hardly allow the merit they fhould be granted, vi. 1. [328].

Prejudices in *disfavour* generally fix deeper than Prejudice in *favour*, vi. 306. [vii. 233].

Whenever we approve, we can find an hundred reafons to juftify our approbation ; and whenever we diflike, we can find a thoufand to juftify our diflike, vi. 256. [viii. 181].   [*See* Love.   Lover.

Pride.

P RIDE, in people of birth and fortune, is not only mean, but needlefs, i. 186. [193].

Diftinction and quality may be prided in, by thofe to whom it is a *new* thing, *ibid*.

The contempt a proud great perfon brings on himfelf, is a counterbalance for his greatnefs, *ibid*.

It is fometimes eafier to lay a proud man under obligation, than to get him to acknowledge it, i. 322. [ii. 13].

Pride ever muft, and ever will, provoke contempt, i. 186. [ii. 13].

There may be fuch an haughtinefs in fubmiffion, as may entirely invalidate the fubmiffion, ii. 72. [162].

A perfon who diftinguifhes not, may think it the mark of a great fpirit to humour his own Pride, even at the expence of his politenefs, ii. 73. [163].

The page from Richardson's *Collection*, shown opposite, is given as originally published. It comes from the *Clarissa* section: the 'Prejudice' and 'Pride' headings consecutive because of their alphabetical listing. (I first came across them more than thirty years ago, and continue to see them – though I've tried to be sceptical– in the clear light of an invigorating hunch.)

Volume and page number refer to both the seven-volume and the eight-volume editions of *Clarissa* produced in Richardson's life-time. The transcription below omits these references. It is otherwise unchanged, save that in order to refer to parallels in Jane Austen's work, the sentiments have been numbered.

Prejudice

1 Early-begun Antipathies are not easily eradicated.

2 Those we dislike can do nothing to please us.

3 An extraordinary Antipathy in a young Lady to a particular person, is generally owing to an extraordinary prepossession in favour of another.

4 An eye favourable to a Lover, will not see his faults through a magnifying glass.

5 Prepossession in a Lover's favour will make a Lady impute to ill-will and prejudice all that can be said against him.

6 Old prejudices [*though once seemingly removed*] easily recur.

7 To those we love not we can hardly allow the merit they should be granted.

8 Prejudices in *disfavour* generally fix deeper than Prejudice in *favour.*

9 Whenever we approve, we can find an hundred reasons to justify our approbation; whenever we dislike, we can find a thousand to justify our dislike.

[See Love.Lover.]

Pride

10 Pride, in people of birth and fortune, is not only mean, but needless.

11 Distinction and quality may be prided in, by those to whom it is a *new* thing.

12 The contempt a proud great person brings on himself, is a counterbalance for his greatness.

13 It is sometimes easier to lay a proud man under obligation, than to get him to   acknowledge it.

14 Pride ever must, and ever will, provoke contempt.

15 There may be such an haughtiness in submission, as may entirely invalidate the submission.

16 A person who distinguishes not, may think it the mark of a great spirit to humour his own Pride, even at the expense of his politeness.

17 It is to be feared there are more good and laudable actions owing to Pride, than to Virtue.

*

A quick look at Darcy and Elizabeth Bennet: all quotations are either from the Richardson lists above or from *Pride and Prejudice*. Jane Austen presumably chose this title (as with 'Sense and Sensibility') because she liked the impact of the phrase. 'Pride and Prejudice' has the effect either of a beginning or an answer. 'Prejudice and Pride', on the other hand, sounds like an ending if one drops one's voice (and, if one raises it), the second half of a blank verse line.

In the novel, we soon see that 'Pride ever must, and ever will, provoke contempt' [**14**]. Though Mrs Bennet is far from being a reliable judge, she is expressing a generally-agreed opinion in saying of Darcy on brief acquaintance:

He is a most disagreeable, horrid man, not at all worth pleasing. So high and so conceited that there was no enduring him! He walked here, and he walked there, fancying himself so very great!

Though, according to Charlotte Lucas, Darcy can hardly help himself:

His pride does not offend *me* so much as pride often does, because there is an excuse for it. One cannot wonder that so very fine a young man, with family, fortune, every thing in his favour, should think highly of himself.

Richardson's view is severer than Miss Lucas's: 'Pride, in people of birth and fortune, is not only mean, but needless' [10]. This attitude, you may agree, is nearer to that in *Pride and Prejudice* as a whole. But, in any case, this lady's judgment is suspect. Her leniency towards those who 'think highly of themselves' will enable her to marry Mr Collins.

A clearer-cut example of [10] is Darcy's aunt, Lady Catherine de Burgh, the dragon-lady and snob whom Elizabeth memorably defeats. Though Mr Collins finds Lady Catherine affable rather than proud:

…'You may imagine that I am happy on every occasion to offer those delicate compliments which are always acceptable to ladies…These are the kind of little things, which please her Ladyship, and it is the sort of attention which I conceive myself peculiarly bound to pay.'

It is a necessary but not a sufficient condition of being sensible that a character, or a reader, should hold the opposite opinion to anything propounded by Mr Collins. Elizabeth Bennet's judgment is sound in this respect, but otherwise patchy. She takes against Bingley's sisters. Her initial reaction may be justified, but, as 'Early-begun antipathies are not easily eradicated' [1], her provisional disapproval acquires a self-indulgent permanence:

> ...their indifference towards Jane when not immediately before them, restored Elizabeth to the enjoyment of all her original dislike.

Elizabeth is wrong to take pleasure in the accuracy of her judgment, when she should primarily feel her sister's pain. In cases of such willed antipathy, 'Those we dislike can do nothing to please us' [2]: a maxim which approximates to Darcy's early effect on Elizabeth, who 'liked him too little to care for his approbation.'

'The contempt a proud great person brings on himself, is a counter-balance for his greatness' [12] serves to point up the unconscious irony in Darcy's account of himself to Elizabeth:

> 'It has been the study of my life to avoid those weaknesses which often expose a strong understanding to ridicule.'
> 'Such as vanity and pride.'
> 'Yes, vanity is a weakness indeed. But pride – where there is a real superiority of mind, pride will be always under good regulation.'

Thus Darcy, having invited ridicule by his effort to avoid it, makes a ponderous response to Elizabeth's needling. Nevertheless, it is a reflection on Elizabeth that she cannot take this serious man seriously.

Worse, Elizabeth has become sure that Darcy is incapable of virtuous action, that even his pride will let him down, lead him to baseness by default: 'he should have been too proud to be dishonest,' she exclaims to the supposedly-wronged Wickham; an account of motivation very much after Richardson, who accepted that base attributes could give rise to the show and effect of goodness: 'It is to be feared that there are more good and laudable actions owing to Pride than to Virtue' [17].

Wickham has become something of a hero to her, Darcy a villain, for 'An extraordinary Antipathy in a young Lady to a particular person, is generally owing to an extraordinary pre-possession in favour of another' [3]. As when Wickham absents himself from the Netherfield ball,

> Every feeling of displeasure against [Darcy] was so sharpened by immediate disappointment, that she could hardly reply with tolerable civility to the polite inquiries which he directly afterwards approached to make.

Thus do 'Old prejudices (though once seemingly removed) easily recur' [6].

Similarly, two paragraphs later, Elizabeth rounds on Charlotte Lucas for suggesting that Mr Darcy could be agreeable company:

> 'Heaven forbid! *That* would be the greatest misfortune of all! – To find a man agreeable whom one is determined to hate! – Do not wish me such an evil.'

This exclamation, with its acknowledgement of her own wilfulness, is the nearest Elizabeth Bennet has come to understanding herself for some time. For 'Prejudices in *disfavour* generally fix deeper than Prejudice in *favour*' [8].

Even good-natured Jane Bennet comes to recognise that Wickham is a scoundrel before Elizabeth is willing to. To Jane's observation ('I am afraid he has been imprudent, and has deserved to lose Mr Darcy's regard.'), Elizabeth resolves almost surlily, 'still to think of both gentlemen as I did before.' In Richardson's terms, 'Whenever we approve, we can find a hundred reasons to justify our approbation; and whenever we dislike, we can find a thousand to justify our dislike' [9].

Darcy seems less objectionable after Elizabeth's encounter with his aunt, the overbearing but undistinguished Lady Catherine de Burgh.

However, Elizabeth's 'old prejudices easily recur', when she learns that Darcy has played a part in keeping her sister Jane and his rich friend Bingley apart: 'To those we love not ...we can hardly allow the merit they should be granted' [9].

Elizabeth, therefore, sets herself to think of him as badly as she can:

> She was quite decided at last, that he had been partly governed by this worst kind of pride, and partly by the wish of retaining Mr Bingley for his sister...Elizabeth, as if intending to exasperate herself as much as possible against Mr Darcy, chose for her employment the examination of all the letters which Jane had written to her since her being in Kent.

At this particularly inopportune moment comes Darcy's first insulting proposal ('In vain have I struggled' etc), which is inevitably refused. For, as Richardson might have written by way of gloss upon the encounter: 'There may be such an haughtiness in submission, as may entirely invalidate the submission' [15].

The Prejudice sentiments connect (through a footnote) with 'Love. Lover.' That entry takes us on to 'Marriage'. 'Marriage' ends with 'Masters. Mistresses. Servants'. Darcy's role, prior to the modification of his Pride, which Elizabeth effects, is primarily that of Master. The first entry here is:
'Judgments of person's tempers are to be made by their domestic behaviour, and by their treatment of their Servants.'

You will probably recall the moment when Darcy's housekeeper, Mrs Reynolds, speaks up for him as 'the best landlord, and the best master...that ever lived.' Elizabeth reflects on this in Richardsonian terms, 'What praise is more valuable than the praise of an intelligent servant.'

＊

To recapitulate: Jane Austen was steeped in Richardson's fiction, particularly *Sir Charles Grandison*. Some twentieth-century critics – if they acknowledged this fact at all – regarded it as misreporting or an aberration, or as having no bearing on Austen's own work. In any event, great care was taken to keep the writers in separate categories: Richardson was long-winded, ridiculous and prurient; Jane Austen was succinct, witty and seemly. The connections between the two tend now to be regarded with more interest.

For present purposes that gives rise to a question. If Jane Austen had such an excellent knowledge of Richardson's work, why would she want to turn to shorthand versions, such as the *Collection* or the Indexes – when the stories were intact in her head? The answer lies in Henry Austen's tribute to his sister, published with her two posthumous novels.

In it, he declares with certitude:

> Richardson's power of creating, and preserving the consistency of his characters, as particularly exemplified in *Sir Charles Grandison*, gratified the natural discrimination of her mind, while her taste secured her from the errors of his prolix style and tedious narrative.

＊

In other words, Richardson's psychology appealed to her perceptive intelligence; while her sense of what was the best kind of writing for her own time made her react against the discursive and impressionistic ('writing to the moment') aspects of his novels. The corollary of which is that she was drawn towards the apothegmatic aspects of Richardson's style, as conveniently packaged in *A Collection.*

A Collection covers Richardson's novels in the order in which they were written – *Pamela* (1739-41), *Clarissa* (1747-8), *Grandison* (1753-4) – with separate alphabetical sections for each book. Those from *Pamela* start with **Address *to the Rich***, and end with **Youth**. *Clarissa* is next, starting with **Adversity,** and ending (again) with **Youth**; while those for *Grandison*, start with **Absence** and end with **Zeal. Zealous.** The 'Prejudice and Pride' sentiments and the others previously referred to stem from *Clarissa*.

     I have found little from the *Pamela* entries that feels likely to have been noted with profit by Jane Austen. The reason is probably its theme of a maid-servant's rise to prosperity and influence – and the consequent aphorisms on social mobility, the levelling effects of Time etc.; with, in the continuation of Pamela's story into motherhood, a protracted analysis of John Locke's writings on Education. These topics are outside the Austen repertoire, except as material for juvenile lampoons; of which 'Amelia Webster' – a miniature novel in seven brief letters – is a fair example. Her protagonist is no servant girl, though the secret post-box in the wood is an amusing variation on the constrained Pamela's constant problems in preserving and transmitting correspondence. This is Austen, her surviving manuscript written in a childish hand:

     DEAR SALLY,

     I have found a very convenient old hollow oak to put our letters in; for you know we have long maintained a private Correspondence. It is about a mile from my House & seven from yours. You may perhaps imagine that I might have made choice of a tree which would have divided the Distance more equally... but as I considered that the walk would be of benefit to you in your weak & uncertain state of Health, I preferred it to one nearer your House,

                    & am yr faithful   BENJAMIN BAR

Comedy came first to Jane Austen's early writing, sentiments a bad second. In her reading, it is likely to have been the other way round.

✳

Sentiments etc Extracted from
The History of Sir CH. GRANDISON.

James Edward Austen-Leigh's *Memoir* of his aunt, though fifty years later than Henry Austen's comments on *Grandison*, is more specific. He tells us that Jane Austen's 'knowledge of Richardson's work was such as no one is likely again to acquire…Every circumstance narrated in *Sir Charles Grandison*, all that was ever said in the cedar parlour, was familiar to her.'

In view of Austen's long preoccupation with this large novel in seven or eight well-thumbed, well-remembered volumes, together with recollections maybe of *The New Impenetrable Secret*, or *Polite Puzzle* in the schoolroom, one would expect it to have been put to demonstrably good use in her own writing. It was.

From this point of view, here is the most pertinent *Grandison* section, consisting of the heading and opening, given in full below – except for the omission of Richardson's eighteenth-century page and volume references. (For anyone with access to those early editions of Richardson, apologies. For most readers, an uncluttered text is probably preferable.) The style and lay-out of the original entry in *A Collection* is, again, after the fashion of page 82, above.

Persuasion. Forced *Marriages*

There may be cruelty in Persuasion, when the heart rejects the person proposed, whether the urger be either parent or guardian.
And still more to a soft and gentle temper, than to a stubborn one.

Jane Austen's title 'Persuasion' was not only unusual in itself but in its kind. Single names of leading characters – *Cecilia*, or *Camilla*, or *Belinda*[1]; and, of course, *Emma* – were the norm for lady novelists. Abstractions or summations were more usually found in drama – Vanbrugh's *The Relapse*, or *Lover's Vows*[2], for instance. *Persuasion*, as the title of a novel, seems out of time. I can think of no other instance of the word, as title or sub-title, other than for Richardson's entry in *A Collection,* above.

The twentieth-century novelist Forrest Reid felt 'Persuasion' to be 'modern – as modern as *Chance, Suspense,* or *Victory*.' Reid was referring to Conrad's novels of eighty years ago. In our own era, there are some single-word novel titles – from Henry Green (*Living, Loving, Nothing*), to, latterly, Ian McEwan's *Atonement, Amsterdam, Saturday.*

To call a novel after a quality or a process, with no immediate context, is perhaps to court misunderstanding. Nowadays, if authors wish to amplify their intention, they tend to bring in an epigraph. By one of those ironies, when I turn to McEwan, his *Atonement* does indeed have an epigraph; and that epigraph is from Jane Austen, a passage from *Northanger Abbey.*

In the case of *Persuasion*, the lines quoted above from Richardson's *Collection* which bear the same title as Austen's novel, could serve as an explication of it. True, Richardson's first application of the key-word is as Persuasion *Into*, rather than *Out of*

---

[1] Jane Austen's choice of novels worth reading and defending (written by Fanny Burney and Maria Edgeworth), from Chapter V of *Northanger Abbey.*
[2] As performed at Mansfield Park in Sir Thomas Bertram's absence.

a marriage. But the passage also contains what amounts to an outline of Anne Elliot's situation, or even of her character: 'and still more to a soft and gentle temper, than to a stubborn one.' Anne's temperament is of course suited to the situation of this late novel. Elizabeth Bennet would have been less likely to have accepted any advice which ran counter to her first impressions.

✳

The first reviewer of *Persuasion* had not read the novel carefully enough to notice that Anne Elliot is no longer 'young'; nor that the title refers to a process rather than the holding of an opinion. He took Jane Austen to task for the line he assumed the book would be taking: 'that young people should always marry according to their own inclinations.'

Nevertheless, he had touched on an authorial uncertainty. Austen had gone as far as re-thinking her account of what 'Persuasion' entailed. Her explanation of the title in the published text was an afterthought. It is contained in the last but one chapter, which her extant manuscript shows to be a re-written insertion.

This is the nub of what she wrote there, the words Austen put into Anne Elliot's mouth (and consciousness): 'If I was wrong in yielding to persuasion once, remember that it was to persuasion exerted on the side of safety, not of risk...' The person who had so persuasively urged caution was a dear friend, Lady Russell: 'To me, she was in the place of a parent,' Anne explains to Captain Wentworth, when the formerly young lovers are finally reconciled.

The book, like its heroine Anne Elliot, is a late starter. It is as if those young men in the earlier works (Willoughby in *Sense and Sensibility*, Wickham in *Pride and Prejudice*), having been persuaded to draw back from Marianne and Elizabeth, had gone on to prove themselves worthy and true. The resolution there, of course, is different – as different as the manner of effecting it. Their stories are acted out. We see and hear of their inconsistencies and depredations: we are able to judge how much credence to put on their fair words and half-truths. In *Persuasion* we are never enabled to see the young Wentworth; that the older, successful Wentworth appears at all looks like happenstance.

Persuasion, therefore, is not easy to adapt for film or television. (One wonders whether there oughtn't to be, in this medium, some flashback glimpse of the couple's initial happiness.) Apart from Captain Wentworth's impromptu letter alongside Anne's remarks to Captain Harville about love and commitment – an intermittently beautiful but stagy section of the re-written penultimate chapter – there is little observable drama. It is a book concerned with memory, intention, inhibition, and the consequences of allowing oneself to be persuaded that someone else knows better than you yourself what will turn out for the best.

Such, then, is the prime sense of 'Persuasion' in the title and the book: to argue the case for relinquishment, to put pressure on a person to withdraw; the act of persuading someone out of something, to cause the break up of an understanding – in plain language, to cause a lady to become a jilt. The word 'Persuasion' in this sense is not in Johnson's Dictionary; though Richardson's *Collection* (same date as the dictionary, 1755) shows it beginning to emerge:

Persuasion strongly urged by parents, is *more* than compulsion (because it seeks to make a young creature accessory to her own unhappiness).

That is Richardson's penultimate entry under the heading **Persuasion. Forced Marriages**, which notes that intensive persuasion is likely to cause more lasting damage than physical constraint. The victim of such verbal pressure not only suffers the consequent pain of the outcome but has *herself* to bear the responsibility for inflicting it upon herself, and to reflect on that.

This section of *A Collection* cross-refers to **Parents *and* Children**, which contains an extension of the meaning of 'Persuasion' to include that used by Jane Austen in her novel. To persuade a young woman (as in the case of Anne Elliot), *out* of an engagement: **Parents ought to be made acquainted with any address made to their daughters, before liking has taken root in love; and while their advice may have its proper weight with them.**

Jane Austen is primarily – though not solely – concerned with the power to disengage (as she herself is said to have retracted a previous evening's acceptance of the wealthy Harris Bigg-Wither). But, though *Persuasion* is not 'about' being pressurised *into* marriage, that earlier sense of the word is also current in the book. Captain Wentworth is apprehensive that Anne may be on the point of marrying someone else. However, his fear that Anne Elliot is being persuaded by Lady Russell (again) to marry a cousin is unfounded.

So, no actual 'Forced Marriage' in Austen's *Persuasion*: the subject is the effects of undergoing what Anne herself refers to as a 'forced... relinquishment'. Austen has shifted the emphasis away from physical violence to what we might call today 'counselling'. The age has become more refined, as have its techniques of persuasion.

A life time before – around 65 years – Richardson's Clarissa is a prisoner in her father's house for refusing a man who is repugnant to her. She will be abducted by her rescuer, Lovelace; and eventually drugged and physically forced (an act which the rake and rapist later asserts could be seen as a preface to marriage).

Even in the five years between the publication of *Clarissa* and *Sir Charles Grandison*, Richardson's own outlook changed – as did the outcome of the latter book, though its plot machinery begins similarly. Harriet Byron, the English rose, is being carried off by Sir Hargreve Pollexfen after his failure to make her go through a form of marriage. Fortunately, Sir Charles hears her cries from Pollexfen's coach, rescues her and puts her in the care of his sister. The complication – for Charles and Harriet are now in love – is that Charles has already pledged himself to Clementina. She is a lady from a noble Italian family, but impossibly Catholic.

The drama of this book has shifted from the still shocking – because brilliantly withheld – and shameful abuse of Clarissa to the inward turmoil and final dignity of Clementina's decision to release Charles from his vows.

The **Persuasion** entry from *Grandison* in *A Collection* cross-refers to **Compulsion**, which has a useful note on the 'persuasion' of Clementina. As usual, I give it in full bar the numerical references to Richardson's works:

In some cases, downright Compulsion is more tolerable than over entreaty. A child compelled, may be hardened, may contract herself within her own compass; but the entreaty of friends, who undoubtedly mean the child's good, renders her miserable, whether she does or does not comply.

Our own choice makes that tolerable, which otherwise would be insupportable.

Persuasion against inclination ought to be considered as a degree of Compulsion.

Had even the noble Clementina been *entreated* to refuse the Chevalier Grandison, in all probability she herself would not have been so happy as she was, when finding herself absolute mistress of the question, she could surprise every one by her magnanimity.

See **Indulgence. Love. Parents *and Children*. Persuasion.**

The last paragraph of the above is Richardson's gloss on Clementina's situation and its convenient outcome, with cited passages from the novel in support. These passages include the following. Square bracket inserts are mine:

> [English lady, visiting Clementina]**'Withdraw, my dear, if you choose to do so, and compose yourself: The intention is not to compel, but to persuade you.'**
> **'O madam!' Said she, 'persuasion so strongly urged by my parents, is** *more* **than compulsion. – I take the liberty you give me...'**

> [Later] **Well, and now, by a strange turn in the Lady [Clementina], but glorious to herself, as** [Grandison] **observes, the obstacle removed, he applies to Miss Byron for her favour.**

The Clementina theme in *Grandison* is preoccupied with the nature and workings of persuasion. The passages quoted – opposite and above – illustrate Richardson's narrative treatment through dramatisation and analysis. Henry Austen thought these two modes separable.[1] For us, for better or worse, they co-exist. There is reason (extractable reason) within the attitudinising, which is also sometimes moderated by even-tempered observation.

Anne Elliot's engagement to Captain Wentworth, and the manner of its breaking, can readily be seen as a re-working of the *Grandison* scenario on a domestic scale. Both Clementina and Anne gain their freedom of choice by rejecting persuasion. The difference between the two is that, after gaining her freedom to choose, Clementina releases Grandison; while Anne ultimately renews the bond. The process took Clementina seven or eight volumes, and Anne the same number of (fictional) years.

[1] See page 89.

It is not that Anne cannot learn a lesson. After all that lapsed time, near the beginning of the book, 'she would have liked to know how [Wentworth] felt about a meeting,' when chance has provided a possibility of the couple seeing one another, in the company of her sister and brother-in-law. But (and Austen's choice of epithet is significant), she is 'quite unpersuadable'; takes instead the option of acting as nurse to her sister's sick child. Being less ready to put her personal life in the hands of others, has given her, like Clementina, a degree of intellectual, though not emotional freedom. But the rights and wrongs of 'Persuasion' are not worked out through any process of dialectic. The book is dependent on chance and the unreasonable steadfastness of the human heart.

That Anne remains in love with Wentworth while having no reason to suppose he still loves her is not the Richardson way. To have this happen – and with a successful outcome – is Jane Austen's final counter to one of her master's key opinions; the end of a process which, in published form, had begun with her only printed footnote.

It occurs in Chapter 3 of *Northanger Abbey* and comprises an argument with Richardson – a man who had died forty years before she began the book. The young Jane Austen here claims the right of a lady to fall in love before she knows that the object of her regard reciprocates her feeling. The later Jane Austen, not only claims the right to continue to love *when there is no longer any prospect of success*, but declares that to be an inescapable aspect of being a woman: 'All the privilege I claim for my own sex...' Anne Elliot says to the sensitive Captain Harville, 'is that of loving longest, when existence or when hope is gone.' And she says this in the presence of Wentworth who is writing his impromptu *deus ex machina* letter.

Jane Austen's preoccupation with Richardson, and especially with *Sir Charles Grandison*, goes back further than *Northanger Abbey.* – to her juvenilia. In the young Jane's amusing dramatisation[1] of

---

[1] Previously referred to, page 11.

Richardson's novel, the uplifting central figure of Clementina is deleted, omitted from the list of characters.

Yet the situation in Jane Austen's closet drama, as in Richardson's novel, is that Harriet Byron will not be allowed to marry Grandison until Lady Clementina is herself safely wed. Harriet's father makes this clear. Grandison concurs. He has held back from paying his addresses to Miss Byron until free to do so. And here comes that freedom, courtesy of absent Clementina. Austen has left her off-stage in Europe, so a letter will have to be sent. In fact, not even a letter. Still further distanced: Sir Charles gives us a *report* of a letter:

> **But yesterday, I received some Letters from Italy in which they have great hopes of Lady Clementina's being soon persuaded to marry. She wishes me in the same letter to set her the example by marrying an English woman.**

This re-writing of Richardson provides direct evidence that Jane Austen scrutinised from an early age the concept of 'Persuasion' through his eyes. True, her view of Clementina here already shows clear differences from Richardson's original. Austen's emphasis is on cheerful propriety; Richardson's on Clementina's independence of spirit – though, yes, in this book, he too is in search of best outcomes.

Thus, Austen already had Richardson's account of 'Persuasion', including alternative scenarios, in mind at the outset of her writing career. Jane Austen's last completed work, *Persuasion*, had, maybe always been on the cards.

✳

A Note on Titles...

The source of *Pride and Prejudice* as a title has become something of a literary game. Instances of its use, or something close to it, have been noted in many works which Jane Austen had probably read. Their authors include: Mrs Thrale, Gibbon, Jeremy Taylor, Cowper, Johnson, Charlotte Smith, Sophia Lee, Robert Bage and Fanny Burney.

Fanny Burney's *Cecilia*, 1782, has generally been the most favoured. Towards the end of her story we are told by a bystander that 'The whole of the unfortunate business has been the result of PRIDE AND PREJUDICE.'

The fact that there are so many contenders, and that Jane Austen had herself already brought the words together[1] before *Pride and Prejudice* suggests that the phrase was a pre-existing tag, perhaps relating to Sentimental Toasting.

My own view of the significance of the 'Prejudice/Pride' entry in Richardson's *Collection* is given on pages 83-89, above. That, and the references to *Persuasion*, are the most interesting Richardson items relating to Austen titles – some of which might also have caught Jane Austen's eye out of context via the cards of *The New Impenetrable Secret*, or...*Polite Puzzle*.

There are others from the cards' source book which should be included here for the sake of completeness. *A Collection* contains possible origins of all the remaining 'abstract' Austen titles: 'Love and Friendship', 'First Impressions' and *Sense and Sensibility*.

First, briefly, in that respect, a single entry from the 'Grandison' section: **Love may be selfish; but Friendship (that deserves the name) cannot.**

This is the kind of text which is behind Jane Austen's early knock-about satire, 'Love and Friendship' already referred to. 'First Impressions' is another such. The phrase is well-known as the title of the lost early version of *Pride and Prejudice*. In Richardson's

---

[1] 'She had seen enough of her pride, her meanness, and her determined prejudice against herself'...*Sense and Sensibility*, chapter 35.

Collection, the 'Prejudice' entry cross-refers to 'Love *at first Sight*', and the following:

> **We wish in compliment to our own sagacity, to be confirmed in our first-sighted impressions, But few first-sighted impressions ought to be encouraged.**

Though there is some interest in fairly close correspondence of Richardson phrases with Austen titles, the citations have more significance. In the above instance, for example, the typical Richardson conflict between self-esteem (unwillingness to recognise error) and submission to those who have more experience of the workings of society and the tractability of the human heart – which is, of course, also a classic Jane Austen scenario.

As for Sense *and Sensibility*, this form of words does not appear in *A Collection*. The sub-heading **Thoughtfulness. Sensibility** comes closest.   Under that heading are five sentiments.

Like Austen's novel, they are concerned with achieving balance between two opposing qualities. Yet Richardson's observations do not particularly resemble the effect or content of *Sense and Sensibility*. Not because his 'Thoughtfulness' differs from Jane Austen's *'Sense'*. It doesn't.

It is the meaning of *'Sensibility'* that has changed over the fifty years which separate the two writers' work. That word retains the core meaning, 'sensible' – sensitive, responsive. But the object and purpose of sensibility have shifted. The cult of Nature, the era of the Romantic poets – with their pleasure in fleeting sensation, and preference for solitude – stands between Richardson's time and Jane Austen's, as it stood between traditional Elinor and trendy Marianne at the beginning of their book.

*

...and One on Lovelace

A correspondent has suggested that I should provide a note on Lovelace, Richardson's hero-villain, whom I have mentioned several times.

Richardson's enormous novels were written entirely in letters – a narrative method apparently followed by Jane Austen in her original versions of *Sense and Sensibility* and *Pride and Prejudice*. As Richardson's *Clarissa* is concerned with arbitrary power (of fathers over daughters and amatory men over females), Lovelace needs to be not only a master letter-writer, but also forger, parodist, diarist, and interceptor of others' mail. The epistolary narrative depends on Lovelace's rapid and brilliant impressions – which Richardson called 'writing to the moment'. Here, is a characteristic breathless account of an attempted seduction over a dish [cup] of tea:

> At last, I will begin, thought I.
> She a dish – I a dish.
> Sip, her eyes her arm, she; like a haughty and imperious sovereign, conscious of dignity, every look a favour.
> Sip, like a vassal, I; lips and hands trembling, and not knowing that I supped and tasted.
> I was – I was? I supped? (drawing in my breath and the liquor together, though I scalded my mouth with it) I was in hopes madam –
> Dorcas came in just then. Dorcas, said she, is a [sedan] chair gone for?
> Damned impertinence, thought I, thus to put me out in my speech.

You will have gathered from the above that Clarissa is a great lady, but that does not save her from being drugged and raped by this man whom she might have loved, and might have made a grand marriage with. The outcome is even today shocking in its context.

Understatement cannot be more understated than Lovelace's terse account of the success of his rape. This is the full text of his letter:

> And now, Belford, I can go no farther. The affair is over. Clarissa lives.

Richardson was much attacked in his life-time (if rather inaccurately) for showing

> minute and circumstantial detail of the most shocking vices and villainous contrivances, translated in the most infamous of characters, and all to satisfy the brutal and sensual appetite.

In Richardson's favour, the point should be made that he creates in Clarissa an impressive, intelligent and resourceful lady – and that while both she and Lovelace are dead by the end of the book, she is not only in the right but has the upper hand. She dies a virtuous death, he is a broken man.

It is worth reminding oneself that Lovelace is the character that Jane Austen started to re-fashion in 'Sanditon'; to render ridiculous in the person of Sir Edward Denham, and (probably, had she finished the book) to civilise.

Richardson was read not only by Jane Austen and her family, but later by, for example, John Ruskin and his parents who used *Sir Charles Grandison* (more than a hundred years after it was written) as a guide to living and letter-writing, as a kind of family code. This book was also much admired by George Eliot. As for *Clarissa*, Laclos' *Dangerous Liaisons* is the most obvious example of its influence in Europe. Many other English and American works, James' *Portrait of a Lady*, for instance, owe much to Richardson, and in particular, to Richardson's Lovelace.

Summary

This work has claimed – with some backtracking – that Jane Austen learnt many of the immediate particularities of her finished work (turns of phrase, attitudes of mind, narrative moves) from the Sentimental tradition, from the work of Samuel Richardson, including his Indexes, and (by way of demonstration) from a piece of ephemera, a set of cards current in her childhood.

It is up to the reader to decide. The first, and maximum claim being made here is that young Jane Austen would have been familiar with the set of 'Entertaining Cards' called *The New Impenetrable Secret*, or...*Polite Puzzle*; that from them, or the source of their text, *A Collection*, or from the source of both (Richardson's novels with their indexes) she, for example: (i) derived all the 'abstract' titles of her novels (Love and Friendship, First Impressions, Sense and Sensibility, Pride and Prejudice, Persuasion); (ii) gained insight into the workings of the minds of a range of characters, including Elizabeth Bennet, particularly with regard to her interaction with Darcy; (iii) took up a specialised sense of the word 'Persuasion' for her novel of that name; (iv) formed the basis of Anne Elliot's character and situation; (v) found ways of seeing and judging – the attitude of servants, for example – outside her own direct experience.

The lesser claim – now likely to find acceptance amongst readers and critics who have read the work of Austen and Richardson in conjunction – is that Richardson is a major influence upon her. (When I was young, the two authors were kept severely apart by commentators, in spite of the family testimony, the texts themselves – and the Austens' fondness for parody and word-play.)

One outcome of producing this book with its reconstructed cards might be that a genuine set would turn up. (I provided a glimpse of one in 2006 in a novel called *Jane Austen out of the blue* – set in 1817 – in the hands of the former Fanny Price, widowed and helping

Mrs Barbauld to edit and write prefaces for the reissued works of Richardson.) I have looked and inquired for the cards for many years without success[1]. Were they to reappear, I would be the first to acknowledge that my own restored set is tendentious – a 'best case' scenario for a putative influence on Jane Austen of Richardson's store of sentiments.

I would, nevertheless, be intrigued to see the real thing. And even if the 100 selected sentiments on the genuine eighteenth-century cards corresponded little with those I have chosen, I would be relieved and delighted to know there was an extant set.

A Collection, source of the Puzzle's sentiments, has never been reissued. Mrs Barbauld, Richardson's first editor, was dismissive:

> It was a vain expectation that [Richardson's maxims] should attract attention, when they were abstracted from all that had rendered them impressive. Yet he certainly did seem to expect that this volume would be used by his admirers as a kind of manual of morality.

My impression is that later, indeed current, critics and commentators have accepted Mrs Barbauld's view with little investigation. I believe *A Collection* deserves reappraisal. It might then come to be seen as having a place in our understanding of Jane Austen, the writer who inveighed against those who sedulously copied out sentiments as part of their business of being young ladies, or even heroines.

---

[1] My inquiries date from around 1970, and include 'Jane Austen and Richardson', lead letter in *Times Literary Supplement*, 17 April 1981.

A Set of Cards
and 'Explanation of the Secret'

The New Impenetrable Secret or, *Young Lady's and Gentleman's Polite Puzzle*

The design of these ten cards relates to the 1758 'Impenetrable Secret', devised by Horace Walpole and kept by him at Strawberry Hill. Walpole's miscellaneous maxims – replete with copperplate flourishes and curlicues – are not presented in a way conducive to the snatched, accurate reading the Puzzle needs. The question of legibility may have been addressed by Withy in his 1760 'New Impenetrable Secret', for the Richardson sentiments used there are described in the launch advertisement as 'neatly engraved'.

The typefaces used for the re-created cards throughout the present work are seen as a reasonable modern equivalent to 'neatly engraved' work of the late eighteenth century. In 'The Puzzle in Practice' narrative (pages 13-67) a clear tabular arrangement is used. Here, in this final section, the Richardson text is fitted into a similar working area to Walpole's prototypes.

Walpole's cards had broader frames – a classical 'egg and dart' frame for the black cards, and an ornate 'link' motif for the red. Though there is no means of knowing to what extent *The New Impenetrable Secret* or *Polite Puzzle* continued Walpole's practice, two of the re-created Richardson cards (with their 'Austen' associations) are depicted in black and red on the back cover.

Production costs precluded the printing of the red cards in colour in the body of the book, so Bill Berrett has designed the frames of the cards to double as descriptive colour-labels.

An electronic version of this section is available to download from www.lulu.com. It consists of the black card faces, with the corresponding red backs – in colour and a larger format. A new brief introduction and the *Explanation of the Secret* are included.

Black sides 1-10

Let a man do what he will with a single woman, the world is encouragingly apt to think Marriage a sufficient amends

Exalted qualities may be sunk in a low and unequal marriage.

It is neither just nor honest to marry where there can be no love.

How unhappy must be that Marriage in which the husband can have no confidence in the love of his wife.

A prudent man will not wish to marry a woman who has not a heart to give.

Marriage is the highest state of friendship.

Marriage is a state which ought not to be entered into with indifference on either side.

In unequal Marriages, those frequently incur censure, who more happily yoked might be entitled to praise.

It is happy for giddy men, as well as for giddy women that ceremony and parade are necessary to Wedlock.

It is not a disgrace for a woman to be supposed to know something.

The same man or woman cannot be every thing that is desirable.

Fortune is the last thing talked about by him who has none: love, love, love is all his cry.

A good estate gives a man confidence in Courtship.

A man may stand a chance for as good a wife among those who have fortunes, as among those who have none.

A worthy woman will not give hope to a man she means not to encourage.

It is not honourable for a woman to keep a man in suspense when she is not in any herself.

A single man may sometimes, in the behaviour of a daughter or sister, see that of the future wife.

A sensible man will address a woman as a woman, not as a goddess.

What additional pleasure must a woman have, who is addressed by a man of merit, and with the approbation of all her friends.

The man who is fond of his own person is not likely to be more fond of that of his wife

Those who have not deserved ill-usage have reason to be easier under it.

Solemn impressions that seem to weaken the mind may, by proper reflection, be made to strengthen it.

Good motions wrought into habit will yield pleasure at a time when nothing else can.

Absence from the beloved object is a cure for hasty love.

People deeply in Love generally think too highly of the beloved object, and too lowly of themselves.

Presence may sooner effect the cure for hasty love than absence when the object is unworthy and the female prudent.

Charity is not extended indiscriminately.

A generous mind, when it grants a favour, will do it grace.

The power of doing good to worthy objects is the only enviable circumstance in the lives of people of fortune.

Where the power of doing a beneficent action is wanting, there is nearly as much merit in the will to do so.

Judgments of person's tempers are to be made by their domestic behaviour, and by their treatment of their servants.

People in low stations have often minds not sordid.

It becomes not gentlemen to treat with insolence people who by their stations are humbled beneath their feet.

A generous spirited woman, to be happy, should take care not to marry a sordid man

A generous mind will love the person who corrects her in love the better for the correction.

A generous person highly praised will endeavour to deserve the good opinion of the applauder, that she may not at once disgrace his judgment and her own heart.

A generous spirit cannot enjoy its happiness without communication.

The man who would be thought generous must first be just.

A generous mind will not take pleasure in vexing even those by whom it has been distressed.

A Person of a mind not ungenerous, will rather be sorry for having given a offence than displeased at being amicably told of it..

111

BlackBlackBlackBlackBlackBlackBlackBlackBlackBlackBlackBlackBlack

Persuasion strongly urged by parents is more than compulsion.

There may be cruelty in Persuasion.

Persuasion applied to a soft and gentle temper has a further cruelty to it.

Persuasion is at its most cruel when it seeks to make a worthy young creature accessory to her own unhappiness.

Parents ought to be made acquainted with any address made to their daughters before liking has taken root in Love.

First Love is generally first folly.

Wise and experienced people will not allow of that sacredness which young people are apt to imagine in a First Love.

The woman narrows her own use and consequence, who resolves, if she have not her First Love, never to marry.

Early Marriages are by no means to be encouraged.

Young people should be allowed time to look about them.

BlackBlackBlackBlackBlackBlackBlackBlackBlackBlackBlackBlackBlack

Love that deserves the name obliges the Lover to seek the satisfaction of the beloved object more than his own.

Love takes deepest root in the steadiest minds.

A man or a woman may have as good a chance of happiness in marriage, with a person of fortune, as with one who has not any.

Love will acquit where Reason condemns.

A prudent person will watch over the first approaches of Love.

It is a degree of impurity in a woman to love a sensual man.

Violent Love is a fervour, like all other fervours that lasts but a little while.

True Love is fearful of offending.

Love is not naturally a doubter.

The proof of true Love is respect, not freedom.

BlackBlackBlackBlackBlackBlackBlackBlackBlackBlackBlackBlackBlack

Is it a necessary consequence that that knowledge which shall make a man shine, must make a woman vain?

A learned woman, with her own sex, is as an owl among the lesser birds.

Men generally are afraid of a wife who has more understanding than themselves.

Women should not be afraid either of their talents or acquirements.

Women who have talents should only take care not to give up their domestic usefulness for Learning.

Young women who are writers, should not suffer their pen to run away with their needle.

Love of reading ought not to interfere with that housewifery which is indispensable in the character of a good woman.

It is the most cruel of fates for a woman to be forced to marry a man whom she in her heart despises.

A young woman will rather choose to distinguish herself by her discretion and prudence than by her wit and poetry.

The easy productions of a fine fancy in a woman confer no denomination which is disgraceful; but very much the contrary.

BlackBlackBlackBlackBlackBlackBlackBlackBlackBlackBlackBlackBlack

---

BlackBlackBlackBlackBlackBlackBlackBlackBlackBlackBlackBlackBlack

Early-begun Antipathies are not easily eradicated.

Those we dislike can do nothing to please us.

An extraordinary Antipathy in a young Lady is generally owing to an extraordinary prepossession.

Prepossession in a Lover's favour will make a Lady impute to ill-will and prejudice all that can be said against him.

Prejudices in disfavour generally fix deeper than Prejudices in favour.

Pride, in people of birth and fortune, is not only mean, but needless.

Distinction and quality may be prided in by those to whom it is a new thing.

The contempt a proud great person brings upon himself is a counterbalance for his greatness.

There may be such an haughtiness in submission, as may entirely invalidate the submission.

A person who distinguishes not may think it is the mark of a great spirit to humour his own Pride, even at the expense of politeness.

BlackBlackBlackBlackBlackBlackBlackBlackBlackBlackBlackBlackBlack

115

BlackBlackBlackBlackBlackBlackBlackBlackBlackBlackBlackBlackBlack

Young women ought to take their rules from plain common sense and not from poetical refinements.

Young women deeply read in romances are apt to find in their own bosoms emotions and fervours in passion.

Reading romances may leave a young woman blind to the qualities of the worthy man recommended to her.

If the second man be worthy, a woman may be happy who has not been indulged in her first fancy.

The finer sensibilities make not happy.

Friendship should never give a bias against judgment.

Two young women who are firm friends should each see something in the other to fear as well as to love.

An error against Judgment is infinitely worse than error in Judgment.

She who acts up to the best of her Judgment has the less to blame herself for, though the event should prove unfavourable.

The eye and the heart, when too closely allied, are generally at enmity with the Judgment.

BlackBlackBlackBlackBlackBlackBlackBlackBlackBlackBlackBlackBlack

BlackBlackBlackBlackBlackBlackBlackBlackBlackBlackBlackBlackBlack

Good-nature is the characteristic of Youth.

Some children act as if they thought their Parents had nothing to do, but to see them established in the world, and then to quit it.

Daughters at marriageable age (whatever some of them think) have more need than ever of the care and advice of Parents.

Modesty never forgets duty.

The loss of a good mother is a call upon the prudence of a worthy daughter.

Where duty to a Parent is wanting all other good qualities are to be suspected.

Children should not be allowed to enter too early into discourse with grown people.

It is not every woman who will shine in a state of independency.

Children's faults are not always their own.

Sweet to a gentle temper are the chidings of paternal love.

BlackBlackBlackBlackBlackBlackBlackBlackBlackBlackBlackBlackBlack

Let a man do what he will with a single woman, the world is encouragingly apt to think Marriage a sufficient amends.

The same man or woman cannot be every thing that is desirable.

Those who have not deserved ill-usage have reason to be easier under it.

Judgments of person's tempers are to be made by their domestic behaviour, and by their treatment of their servants.

Persuasion strongly urged by parents is more than compulsion.

Love that deserves the name obliges the Lover to seek the satisfaction of the beloved object more than his own.

Is it a necessary consequence that that knowledge which shall make a man shine, must make a woman vain?

Early-begun Antipathies are not easily eradicated.

Young women ought to take their rules from plain common sense and not from poetical refinements.

Good-nature is the characteristic of Youth.

Exalted qualities may be sunk in a low and unequal marriage.

Fortune is the last thing talked about by him who has none: love, love, love is all his cry.

Solemn impressions that seem to weaken the mind may, by proper reflection, be made to strengthen it.

People in low stations have often minds not sordid.

There may be cruelty in Persuasion.

Love takes deepest root in the steadiest minds.

A learned woman, with her own sex, is as an owl among the lesser birds.

Those we dislike can do nothing to please us.

Young women deeply read in romances are apt to find in their own bosoms emotions and fervours in passion.

Some children act as if they thought their Parents had nothing to do, but to see them established in the world, and then to quit it.

It is neither just nor honest to marry where there can be no love.

A good estate gives a man confidence in Courtship.

Good motions wrought into habit will yield pleasure at a time when nothing else can.

It becomes not gentlemen to treat with insolence people who by their stations are humbled beneath their feet.

Persuasion applied to a soft and gentle temper has a further cruelty to it.

A man or a woman may have as good a chance of happiness in marriage, with a person of fortune, as with one who has not any.

Men generally are afraid of a wife who has more understanding than themselves.

An extraordinary Antipathy in a young Lady is generally owing to an extraordinary prepossession.

Reading romances may leave a young woman blind to the qualities of the worthy man recommended to her.

Daughters at marriageable age (whatever some of them think) have more need than ever of the care and advice of Parents.

How unhappy must be that Marriage in which the husband can have no confidence in the love of his wife.

A man may stand a chance for as good a wife among those who have fortunes, as among those who have none.

Absence from the beloved object is a cure for hasty love.

A generous spirited woman, to be happy, should take care not to marry a sordid man.

Persuasion is at its most cruel when it seeks to make a worthy young creature accessory to her own unhappiness.

Love will acquit where Reason condemns.

Women should not be afraid either of their talents or acquirements.

Prepossession in a Lover's favour will make a Lady impute to ill-will and prejudice all that can be said against him.

If the second man be worthy, a woman may be happy who has not been indulged in her first fancy.

Modesty never forgets duty.

A prudent man will not wish to marry a woman who has not a heart to give.

A worthy woman will not give hope to a man she means not to encourage.

People deeply in Love generally think too highly of the beloved object, and too lowly of themselves.

A generous mind will love the person who corrects her in love the better for the correction.

Parents ought to be made acquainted with any address made to their daughters before liking has taken root in Love.

A prudent person will watch over the first approaches of Love.

Women who have talents should only take care not to give up their domestic usefulness for Learning.

Prejudices in disfavour generally fix deeper than Prejudices in favour.

The finer sensibilities make not happy.

The loss of a good mother is a call upon the prudence of a worthy daughter.

Marriage is the highest state of friendship.

It is not honourable for a woman to keep a man in suspense when she is not in any herself.

Presence may sooner effect the cure for hasty love than absence when the object is unworthy and the female prudent.

A generous person highly praised will endeavour to deserve the good opinion of the applauder, that she may not at once disgrace his judgment and her own heart.

First Love is generally first folly.

It is a degree of impurity in a woman to love a sensual man.

Young women who are writers, should not suffer their pen to run away with their needle.

Pride, in people of birth and fortune, is not only mean, but needless.

Friendship should never give a bias against judgment.

Where duty to a Parent is wanting all other good qualities are to be suspected.

Marriage is a state which ought not to be entered into with indifference on either side.

A single man may sometimes, in the behaviour of a daughter or sister, see that of the future wife.

Charity is not extended indiscriminately.

A generous spirit cannot enjoy its happiness without communication.

Wise and experienced people will not allow of that sacredness which young people are apt to imagine in a First Love.

Violent Love is a fervour, like all other fervours that lasts but a little while.

Love of reading ought not to interfere with that housewifery which is indispensable in the character of a good woman.

Distinction and quality may be prided in by those to whom it is a new thing.

Two young women who are firm friends should each see something in the other to fear as well as to love.

Children should not be allowed to enter too early into discourse with grown people.

In unequal Marriages, those frequently incur censure, who more happily yoked might be entitled to praise.

A sensible man will address a woman as a woman, not as a goddess.

A generous mind, when it grants a favour, will do it grace.

The man who would be thought generous must first be just.

The woman narrows her own use and consequence, who resolves, if she have not her First Love, never to marry.

True Love is fearful of offending.

It is the most cruel of fates for a woman to be forced to marry a man whom she in her heart despises.

The contempt a proud great person brings upon himself is a counterbalance for his greatness.

An error against Judgment is infinitely worse than error in Judgment.

It is not every woman who will shine in a state of independency.

It is happy for giddy men, as well as for giddy women that ceremony and parade are necessary to Wedlock.

What additional pleasure must a woman have, who is addressed by a man of merit, and with the approbation of all her friends.

The power of doing good to worthy objects is the only enviable circumstance in the lives of people of fortune.

A generous mind will not take pleasure in vexing even those by whom it has been distressed.

Early Marriages are by no means to be encouraged.

Love is not naturally a doubter.

A young woman will rather choose to distinguish herself by her discretion and prudence than by her wit and poetry.

There may be such an haughtiness in submission, as may entirely invalidate the submission.

She who acts up to the best of her Judgment has the less to blame herself for, though the event should prove unfavourable.

Children's faults are not always their own.

It is not a disgrace for a woman to be supposed to know something.

The man who is fond of his own person is not likely to be more fond of that of his wife.

Where the power of doing a beneficent action is wanting, there is nearly as much merit in the will to do so.

A Person of a mind not ungenerous, will rather be sorry for having given a offence than displeased at being amicably told of it.

Young people should be allowed time to look about them.

The proof of true Love is respect, not freedom.

The easy productions of a fine fancy in a woman confer no denomination which is disgraceful; but very much the contrary.

A person who distinguishes not may think it is the mark of a great spirit to humour his own Pride, even at the expense of politeness.

The eye and the heart, when too closely allied, are generally at enmity with the Judgment.

Sweet to a gentle temper are the chidings of paternal love.

Explanation of THE SECRET

In order to know the sentence which any person shall choose, be pleased to observe, that the first letter (which is called the *Catch Letter*) of the last word of every first line or sentence on the black side is one of the ten in A-D-I-S-C-O-V-E-R-Y.

Each of these *Catch Letters* denotes ten red sentences. Thus, every sentence on the black side of the card which has the *Catch Letter* A corresponds to the first sentence on the red sides of all the cards; every sentence which has the *Catch Letter* D to the second line of each of the red cards; while the sentences which have the *Catch Letter* I refer to the third lines; and so through the whole ten *Catch Letters.*

When any person has a mind to choose a sentence, spread the cards in your hands with the black sides uppermost, and in that manner let that person draw one. While it is being drawn, observe the *Catch Letter*, which you may do casually as not to be perceived. Once the sentence is chosen, which must be from the black side, hand the person the rest of cards, asking for the same sentence to be found from a red side. That red side must be returned to you. Once that is done, you silently read, or count, the red sentences down – as A,D,I,S, etc. – until you arrive at the Number of *Catch Letter* you previously noted, which indicates that you have found the sentence which was privately chosen. [1]

---

[1] Adapted from the instructions with the Walpole cards.

Sources

Austen, J *Pride and Prejudice, Persuasion, Sense and Sensibility*, etc

Austen, J 'The Cancelled Chapter', appended to *Persuasion* (ed. Todd and Blank), 2006

Austen, J (ed. Chapman) *Minor Works*, 1965

Austen, J (ed. Le Faye) *Letters*, 1995

Austen, J (play) *Sir Charles Grandison, or The Happy Man* (ed Southam), 1989

Austen, H 'Biographical Notice of the Author', 1817

Austen-Leigh, J E *A Memoir of Jane Austen* (ed. Chapman), 1926

Austen-Leigh (family) *Charades &c Written a Hundred Years Ago*, 1895

Barbauld, A L 'On the Origin and Progress of Novel-writing' and 'Richardson', from *The British Novelists*, 1820

Burney, F *Diary of Frances Burney*, 1889

'Exeter Working Papers', *London Book Trades of the Later 18th Century*, 2007

Johnson, S (ed. Bate et al) *The Rambler*, 1969

Richardson, S *A Collection of the Moral and Instructive Sentiments, Maxims, Cautions and Reflexions, Contained in the Histories of Pamela, Clarissa, and Sir Charles Grandison...*,1755

Richardson, S *Clarissa*, all editions from 1757 (3rd) to 1820

Richardson, S *Sir Charles Grandison*, 1753 (1st), 1770, 1783, 1820

Sale, W M Jr *Samuel Richardson: A Bibliographical Record*, 1936

Southam, B (ed.) *Jane Austen: the Critical Heritage*, 1968

Tomalin, C *Jane Austen: A Life*, 1997

Walpole, H *The Impenetrable Secret*, 17-?

Walpole, H (ed. Toynbee) *Journal of the Printing Office at Strawberry Hill*, 1923

Walpole, H (ed Hadley) *Selected Letters*, 1926